# Kappa

石 白 賀
文 佳 兰

Ryūnosuke Akutagawa

# Kappa

## A Novel

Translated from the Japanese by
GEOFFREY BOWNAS
With an Introduction by G. H. Healey

CHARLES E. TUTTLE COMPANY
*Rutland, Vermont & Tokyo, Japan*

Originally published in Japanese as *Kappa*

Published by the Charles E. Tuttle Company, Inc., of
Rutland, Vermont and Tokyo, Japan, with editorial
offices at Suido 1-chome, 2-6, Bunkyo-ku, Tokyo, Japan,
by special arrangement with Peter Owen Limited,
London.

Library of Congress Catalog Card No. 79-157260
International Standard Book No. 0-8048-0994-1

First Tuttle edition published 1971
Third printing, 1974

0293-000245-4615
PRINTED IN JAPAN

# Note on Names

Names in the text are given in the usual Japanese order; family name first, given name second. Thus, in Akutagawa Ryūnosuke, Akutagawa is the family name and Ryūnosuke the given name.

Japanese writers commonly adopt a *gō*, or pen-name, which replaces the given name. Natsume Kinnosuke, for example, adopted the *gō* Sōseki. It is usual to refer to a writer by his *gō*, if he has one; Sōseki, (Nagai) Kafū, or by his family name if he has not: Kikuchi (Kan), Kume (Masao). Akutagawa, however, is usually referred to by his given name.

0 - inauspicious birthdate
1 - lived in foreign settlement,
   only 2 other Jap. families

2 - temperamental, aggressive

3 - father - violent, argumentative
   mother - timid, schizophrenic

4 - depressed
5 - Edo period literature


Bag — fisherman
Chak — dr.
Lag — young poet
Tok — old poet
Krabach — composer
Gael — capitalist
Mag — narrator

# Introduction

Akutagawa Ryūnosuke was born on 1 March 1892, in Irifunechō, a district of what was then the Borough of Kyōbashi, in Tokyo. He was the last of the three children born to Niihara Toshizō and his first wife, Fuku. Of the other two children, both girls, only the younger, Hisa, survived, her sister Hatsu having died of meningitis about a year before Ryūnosuke's birth.

In those days, foreign residents in Japan were permitted to live only in certain areas designated Foreign Settlements. The part of Irifunechō in which Ryūnosuke was born lay within the confines of the Tsukiji Foreign Settlement and only two other Japanese families lived in the immediate neighbourhood. It was the presence of foreigners that had attracted Niihara Toshizō there : he was a dairyman, and the demand for milk, butter and cream (still somewhat exotic foods to the Japanese) was greatest in the foreign community.

Toshizō had been born in Western Japan in 1851. In 1868, the Tokugawa Shōgunate collapsed and power was restored to the Emperor. Toshizō fought as a young man in the Boshin War of that year, in which the adherents of the old regime were defeated by the armies of the new Imperial Government. He later worked for some years on a dairy farm at Hakone before setting up in business for himself in Irifunechō in 1883. He was an energetic and enterprising man, and he prospered. By the time of Ryūnosuke's birth, he was the owner of five dairies.

But the vigour of his nature also manifested itself in less admirable ways. He had a violent temper and was involved in frequent quarrels. In a memoir of his father written in 1926 Ryūnosuke recounts an incident that illuminates this facet of his father's character :

Once when I was in the third year at Middle School I took my father on at wrestling. I sent him sprawling with my favourite throw, the ōsotogari. He sprang up and said, advancing on me, 'Another go !' I threw him again, with no trouble at all. He rushed at me a third time, his expression furious : 'Another go !' My aunt, who was watching . . . frowned at me . . . and when we closed I purposely fell on my back. (*Tenkibo,* Chikuma Shobō 3, 307–8.)*

Toshizō was a commoner, but his wife, Fuku, came from the warrior class which had dominated Japanese society for centuries. Since the Restoration, the samurai had been deprived of the privileged position they had held under the Shōgunate. Many of them had been forced into occupa-

* References are to the eight-volume *Akutagawa Ryūnosuke Zenshū* (Works of Akutagawa Ryūnosuke) published by Chikuma Shobō, Tokyo, 1964–65.

tions they considered beneath their dignity : they had joined the new conscript army, or become policemen, or entered trade. In name, however, they still formed a distinct class, and had considerable pride in their ancestry. According to one of Ryūnosuke's biographers (his cousin Kuzumaki Yoshitoshi) Fuku's family, the Akutagawas, looked down on Toshizō as a parvenu.

Fuku was a slender, graceful woman, and was regarded as something of a beauty. Temperamentally, she was quite unlike her husband, and life with him cannot have been easy for her. Her younger daughter, Hisa, remembered her as an extremely timid woman who spoke little and was inclined to conceal her feelings. But she was more than merely diffident. Her withdrawn-ness was the emotional self-defence of a schizoid personality, the deterioration of which was precipitated by two events : Hatsu's death and Ryūnosuke's birth. The death of her elder daughter was a blow that Fuku was in any case particularly ill-equipped to withstand, and its effect on her was worsened by self-recrimination, for she believed that the meningitis of which Hatsu had died had developed from a cold the child had caught while the two of them were out for the day together. Within a few months of Hatsu's death, Fuku had become pregnant again. This pregnancy was a source of deep anxiety to her, for what may appear a rather curious reason. This was that the birth would take place in 1892, the thirty-third year of her life and the forty-second of her husband's. A woman's thirty-third year and a man's forty-second were regarded by the superstition of the day as periods of great danger, so that there could hardly have been a less auspicious time for the birth of a child. Ryūnosuke's parents

9

were concerned enough to take steps to avert the threatened ill luck. After his birth, they formally 'abandoned' him. He was 'taken in' by Matsumura Senjirō, an old friend of Toshizō's who managed one of his dairies. It was then possible for him to be accepted back into the family as though he were a foundling, the unfortunate circumstances of his birth thus neutralized.

These unhappy experiences were enough to loosen Fuku's already precarious hold on reality, and a few months after Ryūnosuke's birth she lapsed into a schizophrenic state from which she never recovered, although she lived on for another ten years.

Ryūnosuke, of course, only knew her as she was after she had become ill. In 1926 he wrote this description of her :

My mother was a madwoman. . . . She used to sit alone in the house at Shiba, her hair in a bun held by a comb, puffing at a long pipe. She was a small woman, with a small face that was somehow grey and entirely without animation. . . . I remember that on one occasion when I went upstairs with my foster-mother to say hello to her, all of a sudden she hit me on the head with her pipe. But she was usually a very placid lunatic. When my sister or I pestered her to, she would draw pictures for us on sheets of writing paper. . . . But the people she drew all had foxes' faces. (*Tenkibo*, Chikuma Shobō 3, 305.)

His mother's madness, and the fear that he might have inherited it, preyed on Ryūnosuke's mind throughout his life. Bad heredity is one of the objects of his satire in *Kappa* :

10

There was a huge poster at a street corner. The lower half of the poster showed figures of a dozen or so Kappas; some of these figures were blowing trumpets, others brandished swords. The whole of the rest of the surface of the poster was taken up by writing in Kappa script; it is not an attractive form of script—it is spiral and looks for all the world like so many watch springs. I think I've got the broad gist of what these spiral characters said, though here again there could well be mistakes of detail, I'm afraid. At any rate, I did my best under the circumstances :

> Let's recruit our Heredity Volunteer Troop
> Let all hale and hearty Kappas
> Marry unsound and unhealthy Kappas
> To eradicate evil heredity. (See pp. 62–3.)

Since Fuku was no longer capable of looking after her children, Ryūnosuke was put into the care of her elder brother Akutagawa Michiaki and his wife Tomo, who were themselves childless. He was brought up as Michiaki's son, but was not formally adopted into the Akutagawa family until 1904, two years after his mother's death.

The characters of Ryūnosuke's father and foster-father could hardly have been more different. Unlike the irascible Toshizō, Michiaki was a large, sedate man who always smiled faintly as he talked. He evidently lacked Toshizō's energy and commercial acumen : after his retirement from the Civil Service in 1904 he embarked on several business ventures, all of which failed.

His wife, Tomo, was remembered by one of Ryūnosuke's

friends (Tsunetō Kyō) as kindly and soft-spoken. She was the niece of Saiki Kōi, a famous aesthete of the late Edo period.

The place of Ryūnosuke's mother, however, was taken not by Tomo but by Michiaki's unmarried sister, Ryūnosuke's Aunt Fuki. Fuki remained a spinster all her life. She was a dominating woman, and Ryūnosuke's relationship with her as he grew up was very close. It was also a complicated relationship : he wrote that he loved her more than anyone else but constantly quarrelled with her; that he owed her more than anyone else but that she had made his life a misery. Undoubtedly, her influence on him was greater than that of any other member of the family. 'If it had not been for my aunt', he wrote, 'I do not know whether I should be the sort of person I am today.' (*Bungakusuki no Katei kara*, Chikuma Shobō 4,163.)

In a fragment of autobiographical fiction written towards the end of his life, Ryūnosuke describes the household in which he spent his childhood :

Shinsuke's family was poor, but it was not the poverty of the lowest classes, crowded together in their tenements; it was the poverty of the lower middle classes, who are obliged to suffer even greater hardships in order to keep up appearances. Apart from the interest on some savings, his father, a retired government official, had only a pension of five hundred *yen* a year on which to keep a household of five people and a maid. The pursuit of economies was relentless. . . . New clothes were few and far between, and his father made do at supper with an inferior wine that he would not have offered to a

12

guest. His mother wore a coat to conceal her patched *obi*. And Shinsuke too—Shinsuke still remembers that desk of his that smelt of varnish. Although it was a second-hand desk, it looked at first glance very trim with a piece of green baize stuck on top and shiny silver mountings on the drawers. But the baize was very thin, and the drawers always stuck. More than a desk, it was a symbol of the household—a symbol of the life of a household in which appearances had to be kept up at all costs. . . .

Shinsuke hated this poverty . . . he hated all the shabbiness of the house—the old *tatami*, the dim lamps, the peeling screens with their design of ivy-leaves. . . . But more than the shabbiness he hated the deceitfulness that sprang from poverty. His mother would take relatives gifts of cake in boxes from the 'Fūgetsu' confectionary, but the contents . . . would have been bought at the local cake-shop. (*Daidōji Shinsuke no Hansei*, Chikuma Shobō 3, 231–2.)

This melancholy picture, however, is the product less of the family's actual circumstances than of Ryūnosuke's lifelong over-sensitivity to imagined humiliations and of the extreme depression of his last years. No doubt extravagance was avoided and some luxuries done without, but Ryūnosuke was dressed in silk as a child, and the family was well enough off to be able to keep two maids. The house they lived in, at Honjo, near the Ryōgoku bridge over the River Sumida, was a large one, set back from the street (unlike its neighbours) in a walled garden.

It may be objected, of course, that since *Daidōji Shin-suke no Hansei* is fiction it cannot be assumed that the emotions of its hero are those of its author. But the details of its hero's life correspond so exactly to those of its author's that it is impossible to avoid the conclusion that it is indeed an account of Ryūnosuke's own childhood, recollected in despondency.

In a different mood, he was able to regard his childhood with greater equanimity—to recall with pleasure being taken to see the moving pictures or watching a marionette-show in the grounds of the Ekōin Temple.

The forebears of the Akutagawas were of the warrior class : men of cultivation and refinement who had for generations served the Tokugawa Shōguns as *okubōzu*, functionaries who, among other duties, performed the tea-ceremony for the Shōgun and saw to the entertainment of *daimyō* who came up to court. The family in which Ryūnosuke was brought up was of a conservative cast of mind appropriate to its antecedents.

Japan had reopened its doors to the outside world only forty years before Ryūnosuke's birth, after two and a half centuries of virtual isolation, and was intent on modernization, rapidly absorbing the industrial technology and adopting the political institutions of the West. Within the lifetimes of Toshizō and Michiaki, the first railway and the first iron foundry had been built, and the first modern factories established. A parliament had been created by the new constitution promulgated in 1889, and the first general election had been held in 1890.

Akutagawa Michiaki was an official of the Public Works Department of the City of Tokyo, and might have served as a model for the citizen of the new Japan. There is a photograph of him in steel-rimmed spectacles, wing collar

14

and aldermanic watch-chain that might be that of the corresponding official in Manchester or Birmingham in the year of Queen Victoria's Diamond Jubilee.

But his home life remained almost untouched by Western customs. At home, he wore Japanese dress, as his wife and sister did. His house (which was rebuilt in 1895—Ryūnosuke's earliest memory was of the demolition of the old house in which his grandparents had lived) was of the traditional kind : a wooden structure with floors of thick straw mats, the rooms divided by sliding screens. His tastes were those of the cultured son of Edo (renamed Tokyo in 1868, when it became the capital), a city of which its inhabitants complacently said that to be born in Edo, to be born a man, and to eat the first bonito of the season were life's three greatest joys. His recreations were playing *go*, a game as difficult to master as chess; composing *haiku*; cultivating dwarf trees; painting, in the style of the Chinese Southern School; and carving.

The members of his household shared Michiaki's traditional tastes. The whole family practised together, under the tutelage of a master of the *Itchūbushi* school, the art of reciting the poetic dramas of the puppet-theatre. They went frequently to the theatre. Ryūnosuke was taken for the first time, it appears, at the age of fifteen months : 'I am told that when Kuranosuke entered leading a horse . . . I cried out in delight "Horsey!"' (*Bungakusuki no Katei kara*, Chikuma Shobō 4, 163.)

It was a family that loved literature, but the literature of the Edo period rather than the new Japanese literature that was being created by such writers as Tsubouchi Shōyō and Futabatei Shimei, who were deeply influenced by

15

European literature. In 1917, Ryūnosuke wrote, 'I have often found the material for my stories in old books. Consequently, there are people who think I spend my time searching out curiosities like some old dabbler in antiques. But not so. As a result of the old-fashioned education I received as a child, I have always read books that have little to do with the present day.' (*Watakushi to Sōsaku*, Chikuma Shobō 5, 347.) The family bookcases were full of *Kusazōshi*, the popular illustrated storybooks of the Edo period, and Ryūnosuke read them avidly. The first 'real novel' he read when he graduated from these storybooks was probably, he later recalled, Izumi Kyōka's *Bake Ichō*. But the favourite books of his childhood were the two famous Chinese novels that are called in Japanese *Saiyūki* (Wu Ch'eng En's *Hsi Yu Chi*) and *Suikoden* (the *Shui Hu Chuan*). 'Best loved of the books I read as a child', he wrote in 1920, 'was *Saiyūki*; and it is still my favourite. As an allegory I think that there is not so great a masterpiece in the whole of Western literature. Even the renowned *Pilgrim's Progress* falls far short of it. *Suikoden* was another of my favourites. I still read that, too. I once learned by heart all the names of the Hundred-and-Eight Heroes of the *Suikoden*.' (*Aidokusho no Inshō*, Chikuma Shobō 5, 426.)

Their fondness for artistic pursuits meant that when Ryūnosuke decided as a young man on a literary career he encountered no opposition from his family. 'No-one ever opposed my wish to become a writer,' he recalled, 'for my parents and my aunt were very fond of literature. Indeed, I might well have been opposed if I had said I wanted to be a businessman or an engineer.' (*Bungakusuki no Katei kara*, Chikuma Shobō 4, 163.)

16

Not only his love of literature but also that taste for the weird and grotesque that reveals itself in his writings was acquired in childhood. The *kusazōshi* that were his earliest reading were often illustrated with lurid pictures of goblins and monsters. Tales of ghosts (which were still widely believed in) were commonplace. Ryūnosuke was told by an old woman, who had been his grandparents' maid, how 'this singing-teacher was haunted by the vengeful spirit of her husband, or how that old woman was tormented by the ghost of her daughter-in-law.' (*Tsuioku*, Chikuma Shobō 4, 390.) One result of hearing such stories was that 'somewhere between dream and reality' he saw ghosts himself.

He was a sickly child, particularly subject, until the age of nine or so, to convulsions. His sister remembered his being carried to a nearby doctor's house one night when he was overcome by one of these attacks. He was also nervous and easily frightened. He went in fear of a little shrine the family kept which consisted of a pair of earthenware *tanuki* (raccoon-dogs, animals credited in Japanese folklore with extraordinary powers) seated on a red cushion. And the family's Buddhist mortuary tablets, with their blackened gold leaf, were equally terrible objects to him.

In 1897, at the age of five, Ryūnosuke had begun to attend the kindergarten attached to the Kōtō Primary School, which stood next to the Ekōin Temple, just across the street from his home, and in 1898 had moved up into the Primary School itself. Long before he left in 1905 he had become a voracious reader, spending much of his time in the city's public libraries and the commercial lending-libraries around his home. He would often take a packed

17

lunch with him and pass the whole day in the Ōhashi Library at Kudan or the Imperial Library at Ueno.

It was also while he was still at Primary School that his literary creativity first showed itself. When he was about ten, he and a group of classmates began to produce a little magazine which they circulated among their families and friends. Besides writing many of the stories and poems, Ryūnosuke also drew the cover and the illustrations.

In November, 1902, his mother, Fuku, died. Two years later, in 1904, he was formally adopted by Akutagawa Michiaki. That is to say, he relinquished his legal right to succeed to the headship of the Niihara family and his name was transferred to the register of the Akutagawa family. A condition of the adoption was that the name of his Aunt Fuyu, who had been looking after the Niihara household since 1892, and who had borne Toshizō a son, Tokuji, in 1899, was transferred to the Niihara family register.

Toshizō had long wanted to have Ryūnosuke back, and he and Michiaki are said to have quarrelled violently on a number of occasions over the question of Ryūnosuke's return. Perhaps it was the fact that he now had another son that persuaded Toshizō to agree to the adoption.

In 1905, Ryūnosuke entered the Third Metropolitan Middle School, the move having been delayed for a year by his ill-health.

The account of his schooldays that he gives in *Daidōji Shinsuke no Hansei* is very bitter :

"Naturally, he hated school, particularly Middle School, with its plethora of restrictions. . . . He learned there the dates of Western history, chemical equations that he

18

never tested in experiments, the populations of European and American cities—all sorts of useless bits of know- ledge. It was not necessarily difficult, if one made just a little effort. But it was not easy to forget that it was all so useless.

"It was in Middle School, too, that he most hated his teachers. As individuals, no doubt, they were decent enough, but their 'educational responsibilities'—in particular the power they had to chastise their pupils—turned them in- sensibly into tyrants. There was no device they would not employ to implant their own prejudices in the minds of their charges. One of them, an English teacher nicknamed 'Barrel', beat Shinsuke frequently for what he called 'im- pertinence'. What this 'impertinence' amounted to was that Shinsuke read books by Kunikida Doppo and Tayama Katai. Another, a teacher of Japanese Language and Chin- ese Literature, took exception to Shinsuke's indifference to games. '"Are you a girl, then?" he would sneer.'" (*Daidōji Shinsuke no Hansei*, Chikuma Shobō 3, 234)

This account, however, is apparently as misleading as Ryūnosuke's description of his family's poverty. According to Hirose Isamu, who taught him for five years, Ryūnosuke was not only liked by his Middle School teachers but also highly regarded by them for the quality of his work. His marks were consistently excellent—indeed, his results were never less than first-rate throughout his school and univer- sity career.

Ryūnosuke continued to devour books. He read Kunikida Doppo and Tayama Katai, Tokutomi Roka and Takayama Chogyū, Izumi Kyōka and Natsume Sōseki. He particularly admired Doppo, a novelist deeply influenced by Western culture. Doppo was a Christian who regarded literature as a medium of instruction, a tool to be used in the 'criticism of human life'. He was one of the leaders of the Naturalist movement in Japanese literature, which reached its peak during the years when Ryūnosuke was in Middle School. The Naturalists' view of man as the prisoner of heredity and his environment must have helped to form, or at any rate to clarify, Ryūnosuke's own pessimistic conception of human life; a conception summed up in his last years in the bitter comment: 'Heredity, environment, chance—these three govern our fates'. (*Shuju no Kotoba*, Chikuma Shobō 5, 110)

Ryūnosuke was beginning to read widely in European literature as well. He often borrowed books in English from his teacher Hirose Isamu. In a letter to Hirose in March 1909, he writes that he has been plodding through *Rosmersholm* with the aid of a dictionary (Ibsen was just becoming known in Japan); and in the same letter he mentions *Ghosts, The Doll's House, John Gabriel Borkman, The Lady from the Sea,* Kipling's *Jungle Book,* Sienkiewicz's *Quo Vadis,* Gerhard Hauptmann, and the Russian poet Merezhkovskii. He also read, in English, Anatole France, a writer who was then little known in Japan but whose works were to have a considerable influence on his own writing.

In September 1910, Ryūnosuke graduated from Middle School. Because of the excellence of his results, he was admitted without examination to the First High School, where he took as his major subject English Literature.

Unless there were special circumstances, High School

students were supposed to live during their first and second years in student hostels. Ryūnosuke was permitted to live at home during his first year, but was obliged to spend his second year in the hostel at Hongō. This was for most young men a very happy period, when they were free to be as hilarious and irresponsible as they liked. Ryūnosuke, however, unlike most of his fellows, did not enjoy the life. He disliked the rowdiness, and was too fastidious to be able to accept cheerfully the average student's disregard for cleanliness. Nor was the food to his liking. He usually went home at weekends. His family had now moved to Shinjuku, at that time still a semi-rural suburb of Tokyo, and were living in a house owned by Niihara Toshizō.

Several of his contemporaries at the First High School later became celebrated writers—among them Kume Masao, Kikuchi Kan, Yamamoto Yūzō and Matsuoka Yuzuru—but Ryūnosuke had little to do with them at that time. The students fell into two groups, the more serious-minded, of whom Ryūnosuke was one, and those with, perhaps, a stronger sense of tradition, who affected the uncouthness of demeanour and uncleanness of person that were the prerogatives of students, and who hardly ever opened a book. Kume and Kikuchi belonged to the latter faction. Kume recalled that they regarded Ryūnosuke and his friends as colourless and lacking in personality, and Kikuchi remembered him as a very earnest student who always had a book in his hand.

Kikuchi also thought him 'aloof', and it is true that throughout his life he seemed to many people to be remote, even stand-offish. His friends, however (and Kikuchi was later among the closest of them), spoke of him with very

21

great affection, and described him as kind and extremely considerate. Kikuchi was notorious for the sharply-worded letters that he would dash off to his acquaintances at the slightest provocation; Ryūnosuke was the only one of his friends to whom he never found it necessary to write in this vein. The explanation of these conflicting impressions appears to be that there was a clearly marked perimeter to Ryūnosuke's friendship, that although he committed himself fully to a very few intimates he was incapable of extending to those outside this small circle anything more than a superficial and rather distant affability. His conservative upbringing and his own aversion from any easy familiarity inclined him towards a stiff formality of manner. Even his friends were at times embarrassed by his punctiliousness in matters of etiquette.

Kikuchi wrote of him after his death :

He put up a fence round himself, and no one he disliked was allowed inside it. But to those he trusted, and in whom he saw something to like, he was very kind. He would go to any trouble for them. And once he admitted someone to his intimacy he was most reluctant to break with him, no matter how much of a nuisance he might be. (*Akutagawa no Kotodomo*, reprinted in Kuzumaki Yoshitoshi and Yoshida Sei-ichi ed., *Kindai Sakka Kenkyū Arubamu Akutagawa Ryūnosuke*, Chikuma Shobō, Tokyo, 1964)

The closest and most lasting of the friendships that Ryūnosuke formed in High School was his friendship with Tsunetō Kyō. Tsunetō's school career had been interrupted by a long period of illness, and he was three or four years older than the other students in his year. He and Ryūnosuke spent much of their time together, visiting exhibitions and concerts and discussing philosophy. Philosophy was perhaps Ryūnosuke's chief interest at this period of his life. He read Bergson, Eucken and Spinoza, and made an attempt, at any rate, on the *Critique of Pure Reason*. But his intellectual leanings were still somewhat undefined. He later compared his state of mind at this time with that of the student in *Faust*, who longed to embrace all human knowledge. His wish was to become a great scholar, but not quite a scholar either—something between a scholar and an artist. At any rate, a man of 'spiritual greatness'. He regarded philosophy as the highest study, and so plunged first into that. But his knowledge of literature, particularly of European literature, also continued to grow constantly wider and deeper. He read Balzac, Tolstoy, Shakespeare, Goethe, Dostoyevsky, Baudelaire, Shaw, Poe, Verlaine, the Brothers Goncourt, Flaubert. Kikuchi Kan's belief that he was the best-read man of his generation cannot be far from the truth.

When Ryūnosuke entered High School, he had a taste for the 'gaudy fiction' of Wilde and Gautier, a taste that sprang, he thought, partly from his own nature, but that was also the result of his having grown tired of the works of the Naturalists. In 1920 he wrote :

At about the time when I graduated from High School my taste and my way of looking at things began to take quite another direction. I came to loathe Wilde and Gautier and the rest. It was at this time that I began to

23

turn towards Strindberg. My feeling at that time was that any art that lacked the power of Michelangelo was trash. This was probably due to the influence of *Jean Christophe*, which I read about then. (*Aidokusho no Inshō*, Chikuma Shobō 5, 427)

His interest in the weird and the supernatural had grown, if anything, stronger. In 1912, he began to keep a notebook in which he recorded ghost stories that he collected from friends and relatives or came across in books.

In July, 1913, at the age of twenty-one, Ryūnosuke graduated from High School, second in a class of twenty-seven; and in September he entered the English Literature Department of Tokyo Imperial University. Tsunetō Kyō, who had graduated at the head of the class, went to Kyoto Imperial University to study law.

It was at this time that Ryūnosuke first became friendly with Kume Masao and, a little later, with Kikuchi Kan.

In February, 1914, Ryūnosuke, Kume and Kikuchi, together with Matsuoka Yuzuru and several others, revived the literary periodical *Shinshichō*. In both its previous incarnations, in 1907 and 1910, *Shinshichō* had been associated with Tokyo University, and this third series, although it ran only until October 1914, and achieved only a very small circulation, had behind it the prestige of the University and the considerable reputation of the first two series, and did not go entirely unnoticed.

In the first issue Ryūnosuke printed, under the pen-name of Yanaigawa Ryūnosuke, a translation (from English) of Anatole France's *Balthasar*; and in the April issue, a translation of parts of Yeats's *The Celtic Twilight*, beginning

24

with *The Eaters of Precious Stones*. In the May issue appeared the first piece of original fiction of his to be published, a short story called *Rōnen*.

In 1915, two stories of his were accepted for publication by the periodical *Teikoku Bungaku*: *Hyottoko*, which appeared in May, and *Rashōmon*, which appeared in November. *Rashōmon* was based on two tales in the eleventh-century anthology *Konjaku Monogatari*, and was the first of many stories by Ryūnosuke to be derived from such sources.

In December of that year, Ryūnosuke met for the first time the great novelist Natsume Sōseki. A group of Sōseki's former pupils (he had taught both at the First High School and at Tokyo University as well as at various schools in the provinces) met on Thursdays at his house. Ryūnosuke and Kume Masao were taken to one of these Thursday Club meetings by a classmate, Hayashibara Kōzō. Ryūnosuke had not until then been a particular admirer of Sōseki's work, but on meeting him, immediately felt Sōseki's 'personal magnetism'.

Early in 1916, five members of the *Shinshichō* group, Ryūnosuke among them, published a joint translation of Romain Rolland's biography of Tolstoy. They used the proceeds of their work to revive *Shinshichō* once more. This fourth series ran from February 1916 to March 1917. In the first issue, Ryūnosuke published the story that was to bring him to the notice of the literary world: *Hana*.

In fiction, Ryūnosuke restricted himself almost exclusively to the short story. He did begin two full-length novels, but never completed them. Only three or four of his fictional pieces exceed *Kappa* in length, and then only by a few pages.

The stories fall, broadly, into two main categories: the *rekishimono*, or 'historical' stories; and the *Yasukichimono*, or 'autobiographical' stories. Ryūnosuke's writing is characterized chiefly by its detachment. The fashion of the day was for the confessional first-person novel, the degenerate offspring of Naturalism. Ryūnosuke shunned this vogue, but during the last few years of his life, as his mental condition deteriorated, he became more and more obsessed with his own unhappiness and, eventually, with the delusions and hallucinations that assailed him in the months before his death. Between 1922 and 1927, the year in which he died, he wrote a great many autobiographical pieces, but the stories he wrote during the earlier part of his career were, with few exceptions, 'historical'. They were set in various periods of Japanese and Chinese history, and were often based on tales from ancient anthologies like the *Konjaku Monogatari*. Many were set in the sixteenth century, a time when Christianity had gained a firm foothold in Japan, and have 'Christian' themes.

Ryūnosuke's purpose in setting his stories in the past was to place some distance between the reader and the extraordinary events described:

Suppose I take up a certain theme to use in a story. And suppose I need some extraordinary incident to express that theme in the most artistically effective way possible. It will be extremely difficult to treat this extraordinary incident—simply because it *is* extraordinary—as happening in contemporary Japan; and if, against my inclina-

26

tion, I do so, then the reader will, in most cases, find it unnatural, and as a result the theme itself will be destroyed. So, in order to avoid this difficulty . . . I have no alternative but to treat it as something that happened in the past, or in some foreign land, or in the past in some foreign land. (*Chōkōdō Zakki*, Chikuma Shobō 4, 149)

*Hana* ('The Nose') exhibits many of the most characteristic features of Ryūnosuke's work : it is based on stories from two ancient anthologies, the *Konjaku Monogatari* and the thirteenth-century *Uji Shūi Monogatari*; the central incident is bizarre and the central character a grotesque; the style is witty; and the whole is a psychologically acute comment on human behaviour.

The plot is simple. The priest Zenchi has a nose so long that it droops below his chin. When he eats, an acolyte must sit opposite him and hold his nose up with a piece of wood to prevent it from dangling in his rice-bowl. One day, a disciple of Zenchi's learns that noses can be shortened by boiling them and then trampling on them. The treatment is applied, and, sure enough, Zenchi's nose is reduced to a normal size. He now finds, however, that those who formerly took care to avoid drawing attention to the length of his nose laugh openly at him and make pointed references to 'noses'. And he is relieved on waking up one morning to discover that his nose has regained its former proportions.

The story makes two points, one explicitly, the other implicitly. Of the reaction of those around him to the shortening of Zenchi's nose, the author writes :

27

Two contradictory emotions reside in the human breast. No-one can fail to sympathize, of course, with another's misfortune. But should he manage to surmount his misfortune, we now feel somehow resentful; indeed, it would be only a slight exaggeration to say that we even wish we could cast him back into his former misery. (Chikuma Shobō 1, 33)

But the tendency of the story as a whole is to show human beings as weak creatures whose happiness depends on the opinion of others. The cream of this joke, of course, is that Zenchi, who cannot bear even to hear the word 'nose', and who spends hours before his mirror trying to discover from what angle his nose appears shortest, is a Buddhist priest of exalted rank, learned and supposedly close to enlightenment, whose last concern should be with the vanities of this transient world.

Much of the story's humour lies in the addition of sober verisimilitudinous detail to an entirely implausible tale. For example, Zenchi is a man of learning, so naturally he searches the scriptures for some mention of a great man with a long nose :

. . . but nowhere was it written that Mu Lien or Sha Li Fu had long noses. And Lung Shu and Ma-Ming, of course, were endowed with noses like those of other men. When he learned in the course of a conversation about old Cathay that Liu Hsüan Tê of Shu Han had had long ears—How it would have gladdened my heart, he thought, if only it had been his nose! (Chikuma Shobō 1, 30)

Ryūnosuke wrote both *Hana* and *Rashōmon* in an attempt to alleviate the depression from which he had been suffering since the unhappy end of a first love affair. It was because he wanted to write about something as remote as possible and as cheerful as possible that he went to the *Konjaku Monogatari*, a collection of frequently very coarse popular stories, for his material.

Although Ryūnosuke often wrote at great speed, he was an exacting stylist; his stories are finely wrought and highly polished. He believed that the highest goal of art was perfection of form. This concept of art sprang from his pessimistic view of human life. He had come to regard life as a shabby and despicable affair that could only achieve any sort of beauty when refined and polished by art. 'He did not observe passers-by in the street in order to know life,' he wrote, 'rather, he tried to know life through books in order to observe the passers-by in the street.' (*Daidōji Shinsuke no Hansei*, Chikuma Shobō 3, 236.) It was the mood of the *fin-de-siècle* that accorded most closely with his own state of mind. 'In order to know them,' he continued, 'their loves, their hates, their vanities—he had no recourse but to books. To books—in particular to the fiction and drama that Europe had given birth to in the *fin-de-siècle*. It was in their cold light that the human comedy was finally revealed as it unfolded before him.' (*Daidōji Shinsuke no Hansei*, Chikuma Shobō 3, 236.) The European artist with whom Ryūnosuke may be most illuminatingly compared is a figure of the *fin-de-siècle* : Aubrey Beardsley. Their work has much in common : superlative technique; an abundance of decorative detail; a love of grotesques; a sardonic detachment of the artist. There could have

29

been no better illustrator of Ryūnosuke's stories than Beardsley.

When *Hana* was published, Sōseki wrote to Ryūnosuke :

I read your piece and Kume's and Naruse's pieces in *Shinshichō*. I think your piece is very interesting. It is assured, and it is serious, not merely frivolous. I think its particular merit is that the absurdity is not forced, but is perfectly natural, and is allowed to emerge of itself. . . . The style is concise and controlled. I admired it. Try and write another twenty or thirty pieces like it. You could carve your own special niche in the world of letters. (Quoted in Morimoto Osamu, *Akutagawa Ryūnosuke Denki Ronkō*, Meiji Shoin, Tokyo, 1964, p. 131)

The literary magazines now began to solicit manuscripts from Ryūnosuke. He received his first fee for a story published in May 1916. During 1916, he published a dozen or so stories, and by the end of the year had firmly established himself as one of the brightest newcomers on the literary scene. *Imogayu*, published in September, was particularly well-received, and was again praised by Sōseki.

In July of that year, Ryūnosuke graduated from University, second in a class of twenty. His graduation thesis was on William Morris. In December he took up a part-time teaching post at the Naval Academy at Yokosuka, and moved into lodgings in Kamakura. In the same month, Natsume Sōseki died.

There was some suggestion that Ryūnosuke, the most brilliant of Sōseki's disciples, should marry Fudeko, Sōseki's eldest daughter, but he had already, in August, proposed to Tsukamoto Fumi, the niece of his friend Yamamoto Kiyoshi; and it was in the month of Sōseki's death that their formal contract of betrothal was drawn up. Ryūnosuke had known Fumi, who was then sixteen, since childhood. Her father, a naval officer, had been killed when his ship was torpedoed outside Port Arthur during the Russo-Japanese war. She and her mother had lived for some years with her mother's parents, the Yamamotos. Ryūnosuke's friend Kiyoshi was the youngest son of this household, and Ryūnosuke was a frequent visitor there.

Since Fumi was still at school, however, the marriage did not take place until the beginning of 1918. During 1917, Ryūnosuke continued to consolidate his reputation. He published a number of stories in various magazines, and brought out two collections in book form, *Rashōmon* in May and *Tabako to Akuma* in November. Eguchi Kiyoshi wrote a perceptive review of *Rashōmon* in *Bunshō Sekai*. He commented : 'The keynotes of Akutagawa's works are a lucid intellect and a refined humour. The author always stands outside life, calmly observing the maelstrom.' (Quoted in Yoshida Sei-ichi and Akutagawa Hiroshi, *Akutagawa Ryūnosuke*, Meiji Shoin, Tokyo, 1967, p.55)

The literary world in which Ryūnosuke had, as he put it, 'enrolled' himself was dominated by three schools of writing. It stood on the 'tripod', to use Nakamura Mitsuo's term, of the Aesthetic, the Shirakaba, and the Naturalist Schools, although Naturalism as a movement had passed its peak.

It was, in part, as a reaction against Naturalism that Aestheticism made its appearance. The School had its origins in the works of Nagai Kafū. Kafū had spent some

31

years abroad, in America and France, and had come to despise contemporary Japanese culture, which he regarded as a second-rate imitation of the culture of the West. As a result he idealized the Japan of the past and became infatuated with the life of the gay quarters of Tokyo, where the ways of the past survived. His writings and those of his greater pupil, Tanizaki Jun'ichirō, show a rebirth of the taste for the colourful and the exotic, after the drabness of the last period of Naturalism. Kafū and his followers regarded beauty as the highest good, and the creation and appreciation of beauty as the highest goal of life. Kafū's *Kanraku* ('Pleasure') was the movement's manifesto.

The *Shirakaba* School was not a 'movement' at all in origin, in the sense that its members were united not by a belief in a particular philosophy but by a shared social and educational background. They were a group of young men of good family who had been concerned in the production of three small coterie magazines while they were at the Peer's School and who, in 1910, while they were students at Tokyo University, joined together to found a new periodical, *Shirakaba*, as a showcase for their writing. They were conscious, however, of the unjustness of the society in which they occupied such highly-privileged positions, and held radical views on the question of its reconstruction. Mushanokōji Saneatsu, one of the leaders of the group, used his wealth to buy land in Southern Kyūshū on which to build a Utopian 'New Village' where the inhabitants could live together in brotherhood. It was this idealistic humanism, shared by the other members of the group, that set the characteristic tone of the writings of the *Shirakaba* School. *Shirakaba* ran without a break from 1910 to 1923, and was

32

perhaps the most influential magazine of the period. It concerned itself with the fine arts as well as with literature; one of its achievements was to draw the attention of Japan to the Post-impressionists.

Ryūnosuke did not make his entrance onto the literary stage unaccompanied. Like him, Kikuchi Kan established his reputation with works published in the fourth series of *Shinshichō*; and Kume Masao had become known even earlier, with the production in 1914 of his play *Gyunyūya no Kyōdai*. Other writers associated with them in the publication of the fourth series of *Shinshichō* also began to be noticed. Inevitably, they have been classed together as yet another 'school' (the *Shinshichō* School, or the Neo-Intellectual School), although some critics have said that this is simply one more instance of the mania of Japanese literary historians for classification, and that Ryūnosuke has more in common with such writers as Satō Haruo, Uno Kōji and Murō Saisei than with Kume and Kikuchi.

Ryūnosuke and Fumi were married on 2 February 1910. Ryūnosuke was unusual in having chosen his bride. Arranged marriages were the custom, and ordinarily a suitable partner would be found for a young man by his parents, through a go-between. Marriage was considered to be a bond not between the marriage partners only, but between their families as well, and therefore a matter for the heads of the families concerned; and more consideration was given by them to the good of the family than to the happiness of young people. Marriage was often a means of advancing the family's fortunes. This is not to suggest, however, that Ryūnosuke married Fumi against his family's wishes. We may be sure that he did not, for the law re-

33

quired Michiaki's consent to the marriage, both as head of the 'house' of Akutagawa and as Ryūnosuke's legal parent.

Ryūnosuke had declared emphatically in his letter of proposal to Fumi that there was only one reason why he wanted to marry her : that he loved her, and had done so for a long time. He did not want to marry, he wrote, as many men did, for the sake of convenience and his creature comforts. And the genuineness of his love is evident in his letters to her. But he had not freed himself of the dominating influence of his Aunt Fuki, who appears to have taken upon herself the role of the traditionally harsh mother-in-law. The first day of the marriage was marred by an incident that left Ryūnosuke with a strong feeling of remorse. Fumi bought him a present, a potted jonquil, and he rebuked her for squandering the money. 'But it was not his own scolding; it was a scolding his aunt had told him to administer. His wife apologized, both to him and to his aunt.' (*Aru Ahō no Isshō*, Chikuma Shobō 4, 56.) When, at the end of March, Ryūnosuke managed to find a suitable house in Kamakura and sent for Fumi to join him (since their marriage she had been living with his family at the house in Tabata, to the North of Tokyo, to which they had moved in 1914), Aunt Fuki came too.

In the same month, March 1918, Ryūnosuke entered into a contract with the *Ōsaka Mainichi* Newspaper Company, under which he agreed, for a retainer of fifty *yen* a month, not to write for any other newspaper. (Japanese newspapers published, and indeed still do, a good deal of fiction. Many of the most famous modern Japanese novels first appeared as newspaper serials. In his association with the *Ōsaka Mainichi* Ryūnosuke was following in the footsteps of such distinguished writers as Natsume Sōseki, who in 1907 gave up teaching to become literary editor of the *Asahi*.) Besides this monthly retainer, Ryūnosuke received his usual fee for the stories the newspaper published, and he was also free to write for the magazines; but in spite of this he was still not able to live entirely by his pen, and it was not until March 1919, when he became a full-time employee of the newspaper at a salary of 130 *yen* a month that he was able to resign from the Naval Academy and devote himself to his writing. That month, his father, Niihara Toshizō, died of influenza. In April of that year, since it was no longer necessary for him to live near the Naval Academy, Ryūnosuke and his wife and aunt moved from Kamakura back to his family's house at Tabata, and it was here that he lived for the remaining eight years of his life.

He was now at the height of his career. The three years between his marriage in 1918 and his visit to China in 1921 were probably the happiest and most fruitful of his life. In January 1919 his third collection of stories, *Kairaishi*, was published, and in August his first collection, *Rashōmon*, was reprinted; his fourth collection, *Kagedōrō*, was published in January 1920, and his fifth collection, *Yarai no Hana,* in March 1921. In March 1920, his first son* was born, and was named after Kikuchi Kan.

It was at about this time that Ryūnosuke began to make those famous drawings of Kappa that decorate so many of the books that have been written about him. The Kappa, according to Japanese folklore, is a scaly creature about the size of a small child, with a face like a tiger's and a sharply-pointed beak. It lives in rivers and drags animals and un-

* Akutagawa Hiroshi, now a well-known actor.

wary children to their deaths. As long as the indentation in the top of its head is full of water, it can also live on land.

Ryūnosuke, as we have seen, had early acquired a liking for ghosts and goblins and all sorts of weird creatures, but this predilection for drawing Kappa may have had a rather sinister significance. It is a characteristic of the drawings of schizophrenics that they are full of 'mythical figures, strange birds, grotesque and misshapen forms of people and animals'. (Karl Jaspers, *General Psychopathology*, tr. J. Hoenig and Marian W. Hamilton, Manchester University Press, 1962, p. 292.) Ryūnosuke's mother, it will be remembered, drew people with foxes' faces. It would, of course, be fatuous to base any assertions about Ryūnosuke's psychological condition on a single fact such as this. But from the information about his mental state available both in his own writings and in the recollections of those who knew him, a psychiatrist, Dr. Shiozaki Toshio, has been able to draw certain fairly firm conclusions.* Among them is the belief that Ryūnosuke was, like his mother, a schizoid personality. Such traits as the nervousness, timidity, earnestness and ethical hypersensitivity that he displayed are characteristic of the type. His foppishness (he was particularly fond of tight waistcoats) and his irony were perhaps defensive devices. Physically, he was of the slender 'leptosomic' or 'ectomorphic' type that is predominant among schizophrenics. Whether his ultimate mental decline was a deterioration into schizophrenia or not, however, it is now impossible to say.

* Subsequent comments on Ryūnosuke's mental condition are drawn from Dr Shiozaki's book *Sōseki, Ryūnosuke no Seishin Ijō*, published by Hakuyōsha, Tokyo, 1957.

In March 1921, Ryūnosuke was sent to China by the *Ōsaka Mainichi* as an 'overseas observer'. The trip was to be a turning-point in his life. He left Tokyo on 19 March, but became ill on the train to Ōsaka and did not finally embark at Moji until the 28th. He arrived at Shanghai on the 30th, and immediately went into hospital, where he stayed for three weeks, suffering from dry pleurisy. When he came out of hospital he travelled to Hangchow, Soochow, Chinkiang, Yangchow and Nanking and then, after returning to Shanghai, went up the Yangtze as far as Hankow. After a visit to Changsha he went North to Peking, making an expedition to Loyang on the way. He remained in Peking (where he was treated for diarrhoea) for about a month and then set off for home, travelling through Tientsin and Mukden and down the Korean peninsula (then part of the Japanese Empire) to Pusan, where he embarked for Shimonoseki. He arrived back in Tokyo at the end of July. His health, which had never been good, now seemed completely broken. Whether or not this was a result of the stress of his travels in China is impossible to say, but it is certain that he had lost a great deal of weight in the course of the four months he had been away, and was now as thin, as he put it, 'as a praying mantis'. Soon after his return, he began to suffer from piles and stomach pains. His mental health also grew from now on steadily worse. He began to suffer from insomnia. 'Recently my neurasthenia has been very bad', he wrote to a friend on the 24 November, 'and I can't get a wink of sleep without a sleeping-draught'. (Letter to Susukida Junsuke, Chikuma Shobō 7, 337.) While his health was in this sorry state he was obliged to write an account of his trip to China for publication in the

*Ōsaka Mainichi*. The effort required was considerable, and he later came to see the pressure put on him by the newspaper as persecution.

During the next year or so, his work underwent a profound change. Previously, he had always been the detached, ironical observer; but now he became more concerned with his inner life, and his writing became more autobiographical. From about the time of the birth of his second son* in November, 1922, his health deteriorated further. He began to suffer from stomach cramps, intestinal catarrh and palpitations of the heart.

In September 1923 an earthquake destroyed most of Tokyo and Yokohama, killing about a hundred thousand people. Law and order collapsed, and the city was swept by panic. Many Koreans were killed by mobs because of a rumour that they intended to take advantage of the chaos to seize control of the city. As a result of the disorder, local vigilance committees were set up, and Ryūnosuke became a member of one of them. He and his family had escaped unhurt, and their house was virtually undamaged, but the hideous spectacle of death and destruction that the city presented can hardly have failed to have its effect on a mind already deeply sunk in melancholy. A few days after the earthquake, he went to the Yoshiwara and saw the hundreds of corpses that lay by the lake there—a sight that he described as 'a picture of hell'.

During 1924, Ryūnosuke increasingly turned in upon himself and by the beginning of 1925 he had almost ceased to write about anything other than his own experience. He

* Akutagawa Takashi, killed in Burma, 1945.

38

spent part of April and May 1925 at Shūzenji for the water-cure. In July, his third son* was born.

January and February 1926 he spent at Yugawara, another health resort. His insomnia was by now very bad, and his fear of madness had become an obsession. He lived in a constant state of anxiety, which was made all the worse by the fact that he dared not speak about it to any-one else because of his fear of being put in an asylum. He was oppressed by feelings of guilt.

He exhibited during the last year of his life several of the symptoms of schizophrenia : he developed delusions of reference and of persecution and auditory hallucinations (he may have experienced these as early as 1921); he came to believe that his actions were being controlled by some power outside himself; he had *déjà vu* and *déjà vécu* ex-periences. He insisted on keeping his room darkened even during the day, and tried to confine his comings and goings to the hours of darkness. His wife recalled that when he was lying in the middle of the room he seemed to be afraid that the walls were going to fall in. If she left the room for a moment he would be shuddering with fear when she returned. When this fear was at its worst, he would not leave the edge of the room. He also began to suffer from violent headaches accompanied by moving lights before the eyes that he described as 'cogwheels'. The effect, he said, was like looking through cut glass. It is possible that he did not realise that these migraines were physiological in origin, and may have thought that they too were hallucinations, for he was very conscious of his condition.

He could only find relief from his anxieties in drugs.

* Akutagawa Yasushi, now a well-known musician.

39

For some time, he had been taking sleeping-draughts not only to combat his insomnia but also to provide some escape from his fears; and by the end of 1926 he was taking opium as well. His drug-taking may have accounted for the dazed condition in which he seems to have been for much of the time.

Well before the end of this year, the idea of suicide was in his mind, but it was not until the summer of the following year that he finally performed the act.

The suicide of his brother-in-law, Nishikawa Yutaka in January 1927 meant that the additional burden of looking after his sister Hisa and trying to straighten out her husband's affairs (it transpired that he had borrowed money at a yearly interest of 30%) fell on Ryūnosuke, who was in no fit state to accept such added responsibility.

It was about three weeks later, at the beginning of February, that Ryūnosuke wrote *Kappa*. He worked at a remarkable speed : the whole story was written in less than two weeks, and was published in the March issue of the magazine *Kaizō*.

Most of the critics clearly did not know what to make of it. One thought it a children's story, another thought it 'a sweeping criticism of society', a third thought it socialistic. Only one, Yoshida Taiji, appears to have understood that it was a distillation of the author's feeling of revulsion from the whole of human life; and to him Ryūnosuke wrote in gratitude : 'Of all the criticisms of *Kappa* yours was the only one that at all impressed me . . . *Kappa* was born out of my disgust with many things, especially with myself.' (Chikuma Shobō 8, 90)

Some of the satire of *Kappa* is directed against such tar-

40

gets as censorship and capitalism, but the greater part of the work is an expression of Ryūnosuke's sense of the fundamental evilness of human life and in particular of his resentment of his own fate. In the scene of the birth of Bag's child he gives vent to his own fears that he had inherited his mother's madness :

> I do not wish to be born. In the first place, it makes me shudder to think of all the things that I shall inherit from my father—the insanity alone is bad enough. And an additional factor is that I maintain that a Kappa's existence is evil. (See pp. 61–2.)

The picture of a young Kappa staggering along with several others, among them two who appeared to be his parents, draped round his neck (p. 66), is a reflection of Ryūnosuke's feelings towards his own family, in particular to his Aunt Fuki. The description of the pursuit of the male Kappa by the female (pp. 70–73) is said by his close friend Koana Ryūichi to reflect Ryūnosuke's own view of the relations between men and women. The account of Kappa laws (pp. 104–10) is thought by most commentators to have been written with the circumstances of the death of Nishikawa Yutaka in mind. It is the poet Tok, with his views on the supremacy of art and his eventual suicide, who is Ryūnosuke's self-portrait.

Towards the end of May, Ryūnosuke's friend Uno Kōji underwent a mental breakdown. Ryūnosuke described his own response to Uno's collapse in a rather curious story, *Mitsu no Mado*, written at the beginning of June. In it, he uses battleships as metaphors for himself and Uno :

The First Class Battleship X went into dry-dock at Yokosuka. . . . Her friend the Y lay at anchor in the harbour. The Y was a younger ship than the X. Now and then they would communicate wordlessly across the broad expanse of water. The Y felt sorry for the X, not only because of her age but also because she had a tendency to steer erratically (the result of an error on the part of her architect). But in order not to upset her, the Y never referred to this particular problem, and always spoke to the battle-seasoned X in the most respectful terms.

But one cloudy afternoon a fire broke out in the Y's hold, and suddenly, with a fearful roar, she heeled over in the water. Naturally, the X was shocked. . . . The Y, which had never been in battle, crippled so early—she could hardly believe it. . . .

Three or four days later, since there was no longer any pressure from the water on her sides, the X's decks gradually began to crack. When they saw this, the engineers began to hurry the repair-work even more. But the X had by now given up hope. . . . Staring out across Yokosuka harbour, now sunny, now cloudy, the X awaited her fate with growing unease as she felt her decks warping little by little. . . . (Chikuma Shobō 4, 13-14)

There seems little room for doubt that Ryūnosuke's suicide was precipitated by Uno's breakdown.

In April he had written : 'It is indescribable torment to live with these feelings. Is there not someone who will quietly strangle me while I sleep?' (*Haguruma*, Chikuma Shobō 4, 38.) And in the early hours of 24 July he made his own quietus. As he prepared for bed at about half past one his wife woke up and spoke to him. He told her he had just taken his usual sleeping draught. He fell asleep reading a Bible. When his wife awoke again at about six, he was dead. He had taken a fatal dose of kaliumcyanid.

In one of the several letters that he left, he gave as his reason for killing himself 'a vague unease about my future', but it may well have been that this 'vague unease' was in fact a quite specific fear. It is, of course, impossible to make any confident diagnosis of a particular mental illness from second-hand information, but it seems likely that Ryūnosuke was one of those 'intelligent young schizophrenics who have a painful realization of the inner change which is taking place' and 'may justifiably be afraid that they are going mad, and attempt suicide'. (F. J. Fish, *Schizophrenia*, John Wright and Sons, Bristol, 1962)

G. H. Healey

43

# Author's Preface

This is the story of Patient No. 23 in one of our mental homes. He will tell his story whenever he can persuade anyone to listen.

He must be beyond thirty yet, at first glance, he has the looks of a man much younger. Perhaps it is the madness that gives him his youth. He'll go through the experiences of half a lifetime, before he came to this home; how, for instance, how he. . . . No, I think we should do better to leave such details for a while.

He told his story at great length and in close detail as I listened with the doctor in charge of the mental home. All the time he spoke, he kept his arms clasped tightly round his knees. Occasionally he would glance out beyond the window where, through the iron grille, you could see a bare oak tree, with not even a single withered leaf left on the black branches reaching towards the threatening snow-clouds.

He did make gestures to go with his words, but these were few. When he said, 'I was taken aback', for instance, he jerked his head back abruptly, and so on.

45

I have tried to set down in writing the story he told us with as much accuracy as I can command. If there is anyone dissatisfied with my version, he has only to go out just beyond Tokyo to the village where the mental home stands. There, Patient No. 23, looking much younger than his years, will, I am sure, welcome him with a polite bow and motion him to a hard chair. Then, I have not the least doubt, he will calmly retell this story, a gloomy smile playing over his face all the time he is speaking.

Then, finally—yes, I still recall very vividly the look on his face as he came to the end of his story. No doubt he'll do the same; he will leap to his feet, shake his fists wildly and begin thundering away at you: 'Get out! Get to hell out of here, you swine! You bloody fool! You're jealous, you filthy swine! It's bloody impudence, it is, coming here like this! You're on the make, aren't you, you cocky bastard, giving yourself such bloody airs. Go on, get to hell out of my sight, you swine. Can't any of you bastards leave me on my own?'

# I

The whole thing began on an ordinary summer's day three years ago. With a rucksack on my back, I had set out from a hot-spring inn at Kamikōchi to climb Mount Hodaka. As you know well enough, the only way to get on to Mount Hodaka is by following a route along the valley of the River Azusa. I had been on Mount Hodaka before—and Mount Yarigatake too, for that matter—so, even with a thick mist coming down in the Azusa valley, I hadn't bothered to get myself a guide.

The mist wasn't showing any signs of lifting—in fact, if anything, it was growing thicker. I kept up on the Azusa valley for about an hour, the mist billowing round me as I walked. At one point, I did think of turning back and retracing my steps to the hot-spring inn where I'd stayed at Kamikōchi; but this would still have meant the same wait for the fog to clear, before I could set off downwards.

As if to mock my indecision, the mist grew thicker and thicker every minute. 'Ah well . . . I suppose it'd be

47

better if I carried on. . . . I decided; so I started making my way through the dwarf bamboo, taking care not to wander too far from the river.

Wherever I looked, there was nothing but dense fog. However, through the swirling mist, I did catch an occasional glimpse of thick beech and fir tree branches, their leaves dripping and glistening a greeny-blue against the flat light of the damp mist. Now and again a horse or a cow out at pasture loomed up suddenly in front of me; it vanished just as suddenly, wrapped in a billowing swirl of dense fog.

It was not long before my legs grew weary and my stomach began to feel empty. My climbing clothes and the blankets I carried had become sodden in the mist and were a good deal heavier than normal. In the end, I lost heart and gave in to all these hardships and made up my mind to pick my way back to the bank of the Azusa river. I could hear the sound of the water as it drove against the rocks in its bed and this offered reliable enough guidance. I sat myself down on a rock by the river bank and started to prepare myself some food straight away. I suppose I spent something like ten minutes opening my tin of corned beef, collecting a supply of dry branches and getting a fire going. During these ten minutes, the fog had begun to lift slowly and I found I could now pick out the dim lines of the scenery about me.

Munching a hunk of bread, I took a glance at my wrist watch. It was already twenty minutes past one. This was

surprising enough : but far more alarming was the fleet-
ing reflection that I caught in the watch glass. It was a
weird, eerie face.

Startled, I looked behind me to see where the reflection came from. And, for the first time in my life, I
clapped eyes on a real live Kappa. He was on top of a
rock just behind me and he looked just like all the pictures I'd seen of a Kappa; he had one arm round the
trunk of a silver birch and he was shading his eyes with
the other hand as he looked down on me with the
curiosity you would reserve for something very unusual.

I was startled out of my wits, too shocked for a time to
risk the slightest movement. But the Kappa seemed just
as shaken and he too stayed stock-still—even the hand
above his eye didn't move an inch.

I jerked myself to my feet and made a sudden spring
up the rock where the Kappa stood. In the same instant,
the Kappa scrambled away from me. Or, at least, I think
he did. . . . All I can say with certainty is that he
suddenly vanished completely from my sight, the
moment he'd nimbly turned his body round to make his
getaway.

It was all becoming more and more puzzling and
alarming. Trying to get a sight of him again, I let my
glance rake over the dwarf bamboo. Then I picked him
out again; he was a bare couple of yards away from me,
his face turned back in my direction, his body poised for
a leap beyond my grasp once more.

There was nothing surprising about this, I agree; but

49

what did strike me as so unexpected was his colour. The Kappa that had been watching me from the rock had been a dull grey from head to foot. But now every inch of his skin had turned green.

'Damn you!' I yelled, my voice raised to a piercing scream, as I made another spring at the Kappa. I suppose I need hardly say that he got away from me; and I spent at least the next half-hour chasing after him, thrusting my way savagely through the bamboo, leaping feverishly over the rocks.

The Kappa had a really nimble pair of legs—he was no less nippy than a monkey. By now, I was almost in a daze as I chased him. Any number of times I seemed to be on the point of losing sight of him. More than once, I missed my footing and tumbled headlong.

However, it seemed as though my luck might have turned when the Kappa found his way blocked by a bull, grazing just underneath the thick boughs of a huge horse-chestnut tree. The bull sported a powerful pair of horns and there was a savage glare in his bloodshot eyes. The Kappa caught sight of the bull and, with a shriek, somersaulted right into the middle of a clump of particularly tall bamboo grass.

'Got you! Got you at last!' I shouted as I plunged straight after him into the bamboo grass.

But I was not to know that there was some sort of hole just there. I was just getting the tips of my fingers on his glassy, slippery back when I suddenly found myself toppling headlong, deep into a pitch black abyss.

50

Isn't it strange how, even at a moment of such extreme crisis, our human mind indulges in the most preposterous thoughts?

One moment, my mind was taken up with the danger I'd got myself into; the next, I found myself remembering that there is a bridge called Kappa bridge just by the hot-spring inn where I'd stayed at Kamikōchi.

Then . . . I'm afraid I can't remember anything of what happened afterwards. All I know is that I felt something like a flash of lightning pass in front of my eyes; that's the last thing I can recall and it must have been soon after that that I lost consciousness.

# 2

When at last I came to my senses and took a look round, I found I was still flat on my back where I'd fallen, hemmed in by a large circle of Kappas. There was a Kappa kneeling at my side, holding a stethoscope to my chest; he had pince-nez clamped to his thick beak. As soon as he saw that my eyes were opening, he motioned me to stay still and then called, 'Quax! Quax!' to some Kappas behind him.

At this, two Kappas walked up to where I lay, carrying a stretcher. I was lifted on to it and carried gently through the throng of Kappas. Then we went for several hundred yards along a street which, for all I could see, looked just like Ginza, the main street in Tokyo. It had a similar line of beech trees on each side and a steady stream of cars filled the road between them. In the shade cast by these trees, there were rows of shops; these dealt in everything you could think of and each sported its sunshade.

Presently the stretcher bearers turned off the main

road into a narrow side lane and I was carried into a house just beyond the turning. I was later to discover that this house belonged to the Kappa with the pince-nez; he was called Chak and he turned out to be a doctor. Chak got the stretcher bearers to put me down on a neat bed and then made me drink a glass of medicine. I didn't recognize it—but it was, as I remember, some sort of clear liquid. I lay sprawled on the bed, just as I'd been set down, and allowed Chak to do as he wanted with me; for, to tell the truth, every joint in my body ached so painfully that I had the greatest difficulty even in moving.

Chak came to examine me two or three times a day without fail. And another visitor, who used to come in every three days or so, was the Kappa I'd encountered up in the world of human beings; this one's name was Bag and he was a fisherman.

The average Kappa knows far more about us humans than we do about him. This may have something to do with the fact that the Kappas manage to lay hands on far more human beings than we do Kappas. I'm not so sure that 'lay hands on' is quite the proper term; but, be that as it may, there had been any number of human beings who found themselves in Kappaland long before it became my turn, and not a few of these had ended up spending the rest of their lives there.

One of the main attractions, obviously, consists in the fact that we humans can manage to live quite a good life, without lifting a finger to do any work, purely by virtue of the special circumstance of our being human beings and not Kappas. Apropos of this, Bag did once tell me the story of a young labourer (he had been working on the roads) who found himself in Kappaland. He had married a she-Kappa who, for one thing, was just about the prettiest you could ever hope to see and, for another, was highly successful in pulling the wool over his eyes.

After a week or so, arrangements were made for me to take up residence as a neighbour of Chak with the status of a 'specially protected person': this was necessary in order to comply with one of the statutory provisions of Kappaland.

Considering how tiny it was, my home was unexpectedly neat and cosy. As one might well expect, there is no very great difference between the elements of a civilized life in Kappaland and those of a country in our human world—or at least, to limit my statement to my own experience, the components of the cultured life in Japan. There was a baby piano, for instance, in a recess in my sitting-room that looked out on to the street, and framed etchings hung on the walls. The one inconvenience was the size of everything—the house itself, the tables, the chairs, everything in fact had been made to measure for a Kappa and all the time I felt rather as if I had been put back into the nursery.

This room was the place where, every evening, Chak or Bag or another of my Kappa acquaintances joined me in a Kappanese lesson. And, of course, I had many other visitors, for my status as a 'specially protected person' invited curiosity. Gael, the director of a glass corporation, was one of those who dropped in regularly. He had an arrangement with Chak for a daily blood pressure check. But, for the first fortnight or so, it was Bag the fisher Kappa who befriended me most of all.

It was a warm, muggy evening. I was in my sitting-room with Bag the fisher Kappa at the other side of the table. We'd been chatting away happily and then, for some unaccountable reason, Bag suddenly went silent and began to stare hard at me, his big eyes distended so that they appeared even bigger than usual. It all seemed pretty odd to me and, in an attempt to get to the bottom of it, I tried speaking to Bag in Kappanese.

'Quax, Bag, quo quel quan?' (In translation, this would go something like, 'Come on, Bag! Whatever's the matter?')

But I got no reply. Instead, Bag leapt violently to his feet and stood over me, his tongue lolling limply from his mouth. He looked for all the world as if he were steadying himself for a frog-leap that would land him right on top of me.

By this time, I was feeling very uneasy and suspicious. I managed to ease myself up from my chair stealthily enough not to disturb him and was on the point of making a headlong dash for the door just as Dr Chak showed his face round the self-same door. He couldn't have chosen a more welcome moment. 'Steady on, Bag! Whatever are you doing?'

Chak glared angrily at Bag through his pince-nez.

Bag looked very sheepish and embarrassed—as well he might! Then he began to apologize, drawing his hands across his face over and over again as he spoke.

'I truly am most dreadfully sorry for what happened. You see, it really was so intriguing, watching the gentleman grow more and more uneasy. Then I got so far that I was carried away a bit and I just couldn't resist playing this prank on him.'

Then he turned his apologies to me.

'I do hope you will forgive me, too, sir. . . .'

# 3

Before I go any further with my story, I think I ought perhaps to give you a brief description of the Kappa.

The Kappa is a creature about whose existence there is still considerable dispute. But surely there can no longer be the slightest room for such doubt now that I have personally lived among them.

So, let me lay aside any question about whether or not the Kappa exists and tell you about this animal. I found no conspicuous difference from the Kappa as it appears from the description in a book called *An Enquiry into the Water Tiger*; there is the same short hair on the head, the same webbed hands and feet. The average height of a Kappa is just over three feet, and, according to Dr Chak, its average weight varies between twenty and thirty pounds. Dr Chak did also mention that one comes across the occasional well-built Kappa who might weigh up to fifty-odd pounds.

The distinctive feature of the Kappa is the oval-shaped saucer to be found on top of its head. As the

Kappa's age increases, this saucer gradually hardens; there was quite a difference to the touch between the young Chak's saucer and that of the old man Bag.

But I dare say that it is the colouring of the Kappa's skin that is its most remarkable feature. The Kappa's skin does not retain a uniform colour as is the case with us humans; it always changes colour so as to blend with that of the environment. If a Kappa is in grass, for example, its skin will change to a green colour, and when it is on a rock its skin will change to a matching grey. This phenomenon is not distinctive to the Kappa; as you know, of course, it occurs also in the chameleon. It could well be, I suppose, that there is some property in the skin structure of the Kappa which it shares with or is analogous to that of the chameleon.

When I discovered this fact, I recalled that I had once seen some folklore record which stated that the Kappa is green in western Japan and red in the area of the north-east. And I was reminded of the time when I was chasing Bag—his sudden and complete disappearance was no doubt linked with this chameleon-like quality in the skin of the Kappa.

The Kappa seems to have a fairly thick deposit of fatty tissue beneath his skin; this would account for his never clothing himself even in the comparatively low temperature of this underground kingdom, where the average temperature is about ten degrees Centigrade.

The Kappa, as you no doubt expect, wears spectacles, uses a cigarette case and carries a purse or pocket book.

Even without clothes, he has no real trouble in disposing such possessions about his person, for he is endowed with a pouch in his belly, rather like a kangaroo's.

The one thing that struck me as really amusing was the fact that the Kappa does not even wear any form of loin covering. On one occasion, I tried asking Bag about this practice. He threw his head back and guffawed so loudly and so long that I thought he'd never be able to stop. His reply—once he'd managed to restrain himself enough to be able to talk—didn't make matters any better.

'I get just as much amusement from the way you cover yourself,' he said.

# 4

I gradually came to be able to follow everyday Kappanese. This meant that I was able to understand something of their customs and practices. The most puzzling
of all was the confusing Kappa way of getting everything
upside down : where we humans take a thing seriously,
the Kappa will tend to be amused; and, similarly, what
we humans find amusing the Kappa will take in deadly
earnest.

A few instances might make my meaning clearer. You
will agree that righteousness and humanity, for example,
are treated in deadly earnest by us humans; but when
he hears these words, any Kappa will burst into the most
raucous laugh. It seems as if their sense of humour is
based on canons quite different from ours.

I was once discussing birth control with Dr Chak. In
the middle of the conversation, he suddenly opened his
mouth wide and burst into violent laughter, fit to shake
his pince-nez from his nose. As you would expect, this
angered me and I was a bit short with him when I asked

him what he found so funny. As I remember it, the gist of Chak's answer was something like this—though I may well have got some of the details slightly wrong, because at the time I had still not thoroughly mastered Kappanese.

'But surely you must agree that it's quite ludicrous for parents to take only their own circumstances into account. Doesn't this strike you as the height of selfishness?'

But there is the other side of the picture; for, by all human standards, nothing could be quite so ludicrous as the processes of Kappa childbirth. Not very long after this conversation with Chak, I went to Bag's cottage to watch as his wife gave birth to a child.

Just as we would, the Kappa calls in a doctor or a midwife to assist at the delivery. But when it comes to the moment just before the child is born, the father—almost as if he is telephoning—puts his mouth to the mother's vagina and asks in a loud voice:

'Is it your desire to be born into this world, or not? Think seriously about it before you reply.'

Bag followed this regular practice; kneeling on the floor so as to bring his mouth on a level with his wife's vagina, he asked the question a number of times, after which he rinsed his mouth with a liquid disinfectant that lay handy on the table.

Then came the child's reply from inside its mother's womb; it seemed to be having no small amount of scruple, for the voice was weak and hesitant.

'I do not wish to be born. In the first place, it makes

61

me shudder to think of all the things that I shall inherit from my father—the insanity alone is bad enough. And an additional factor is that I maintain that a Kappa's existence is evil.'

This reply considerably embarrassed Bag, who began to scratch his head as he listened. Meanwhile, the midwife who had been called to assist at the birth deftly inserted a thick glass pipe into the wife's vagina and used it to channel an injection of some sort of fluid through to her womb. This clearly had the effect of relaxing her and, in her relief, she heaved a long, deep sigh. At the same time, her belly, which until that moment had been distended, began to shrivel and go limp just like a balloon as it loses its air.

As you may have gathered from the reply of Bag's unborn foetus, Kappa babies can walk and talk from the very moment of birth. Chak once told me the story of a child giving a public address on the subject of the existence of God when it was only twenty-six days old. But the poor thing was dead and buried before it was two months old.

While we are on the topic of childbirth, let me tell you about something that I chanced on when I'd only been in Kappaland for just over a couple of months. There was a huge poster at a street corner. The lower half of the poster showed figures of a dozen or so Kappas; some of these figures were blowing trumpets, others brandished swords. The whole of the rest of the surface of the poster was taken up by writing in Kappa script; it is not an attractive form of script—it is spiral and looks for all the world like so many watch-springs. I think I've got the broad gist of what these spiral characters said, though here again there could well be mistakes of detail, I'm afraid. At any rate, I did my best under the circumstances; I had a Kappa student called Lap with me and he was kind enough to read the writing off to me. As he read in a loud voice, I took the slogan down in my notebook, word for word.

> Let's recruit our Heredity Volunteer Troop
> Let all hale and hearty Kappas
> Marry unsound and unhealthy Kappas
> To eradicate evil heredity

Of course, I said to Lap there and then that this sort of thing just was not practicable, whereupon, Lap himself and all the Kappas within earshot burst into raucous laughter.

'You say it wouldn't work? Yet, from what you yourself have told me, it seems to me that you humans are actually doing very much the same sort of thing. You've got examples of the young gentleman falling for the family maid, the young lady falling for the chauffeur. Now what would you say all this is about? Surely it's the same thing, isn't it—they're all, quite unconsciously, eradicating evil heredity. I'd say that this Volunteer Troop of ours has a purpose far and away more lofty than the human volunteers you were telling me about

63

not so long ago. You remember, don't you, the group of volunteers who were prepared to kill each other, all for the sake of grabbing a single stretch of railway line.'

Lap's words sounded serious and sober enough; but, for all that, I had noticed that in his suppressed merriment his bulging paunch heaved ceaselessly like a restless sea. But even if I'd felt like laughing with him, I hadn't the time—for I was making a frantic grab at one of the Kappas who'd been watching us. I'd suddenly realized, you see, that while I'd been absorbed in watching what was going on, he'd robbed me of my fountain pen.

But the clammy and slimy skin of a Kappa makes it no easy task for us human beings to lay hands on one. This chap squirmed like an eel and wriggled out of my grip and made off like a flash. He knew how to run all right; his body, as thin as a gnat's, slanted so low towards the ground that I thought he'd fall flat on his face at any moment.

Tok — family
society
art.

# 5

Lap did any number of things to help me. In fact, he was
just as considerate to me as Bag. It was Lap who intro-
duced me to a Kappa called Tok—and this was the most
unforgettable of his many kindnesses.

Tok was one of the poets in a circle of Kappa artists.
He grew his hair long, just like our Japanese poets. Now
and again, to help a dull day along, I would go to Tok's
house. He always seemed the picture of contentment,
writing a poem, smoking a cigarette in his cosy room
festooned with potted alpine plants. In a corner of this
room, there was always a she-Kappa, busy with her knit-
ting or something of the sort. (Tok believed in free love,
so he had not gone in for a wife.)

As soon as he saw that it was me, Tok would greet
me with a smile. (I must say, I never found anything at
all attractive about the Kappa smile : indeed, during the
first few months, I found it hard not to feel there was
something forbidding about it.)

'Hello ! How good to see you again ! Do come in and
sit yourself down here !'

Tok would often give me his ideas about Kappa life and Kappa art. The basis of his belief was that there can be nothing in this world quite so absurd as the life of the Kappa-in-the-street. According to him, parents and children, husbands and wives, brothers and sisters—all spend their time indulging their sole pleasure, that of making life burdensome for each other.

For Tok, the Kappa family system was absurd beyond all belief. One day, he pointed through the window and said, almost spitting out his words, 'Just take a look at that! Have you ever seen anything quite so stupid?' I looked through the window. There, a Kappa who was still quite young was staggering along the street, gasping desperately for breath; draped round his neck were seven or eight Kappas, including two who looked like his mother and father.

But it was the other aspect of the scene that struck me most—the self-sacrificing spirit of the young Kappa, which I found quite admirable. So I began finding good words for his praiseworthy efforts. But Tok would have none of it.

'Oh dear! Yes—you've all the makings of a good citizen of our Kappaland, as well as your own country, you know. Oh, by the way, you're a socialist aren't you?'

With no hesitation, I replied, 'Qua.' (This is the Kappanese for our 'yes'.)

'Then, I suppose, you'd be quite happy to sacrifice a genius in the cause of a hundred ordinary people?'

*art*

'What are you, then? Somebody once told me something about Tok being an anarchist, but, well. . . .'

'Me? Oh, no, I'm a superman.' (Actually, the word he used translates literally as super-Kappa.) There was a triumphant tone about this reply.

As you would expect, Tok holds pretty original ideas about the arts. His view is that the arts should not be controlled by anything or anyone: it's a case of art for art's sake, and so the artist's primary concern should be to make himself into a super-Kappa transcending all notions of good and evil.

Of course, Tok wasn't by any means the only Kappa to hold such views about art and the artist; I remember that they were to be found quite generally among the group of poets he associated with, and among the members of the super-Kappa club where he entertained me now and again. Nearly all the members of the super-Kappa club appeared to be connected in some way with the arts—there were poets, novelists, playwrights, critics, painters, composers, sculptors, as well as a fair number of amateur dabblers. But, whatever their branch of art or their status in it, they were every one of them super-Kappas.

If you were looking for a stimulating discussion, your best bet was always the brightly-lit *salon* in the super-Kappa club. It would be hard to find better entertainment than, as often happened, the members proudly displaying to each other their own particular brand of super-Kappahood. Let me give you the odd example: I remember once watching one of the sculptors (I think it was) standing in the middle of a group of potted giant ferns; he had his arms round a young Kappa, and was engaged intently in the finest public act of consenting homosexual adults you could ever hope to see. And on another occasion a woman Kappa novelist was standing on a table showing us how to drink bottles of absinth. She got as far as sixty—but I expect I don't need to tell you that after she'd downed the sixtieth bottle, she slumped from the table to the floor. In a second or two she was dead.

Walking arm in arm, Tok and I were making our way home from the super-Kappa club one night; there was a full moon. Tok was unusually depressed and didn't venture a single word. It wasn't long, however, before we passed a small window; by the flickering light of the fire in the room within, we saw a table laid for the evening meal. Sitting at it were two older Kappas, evidently husband and wife, and their three children. Suddenly, Tok heaved a deep sigh and said to me:

'Just look at me! Here I am, thinking of myself as the one and only super-Kappa lover; but I take one look at a scene of family life like this and I end up as jealous as sin. Ah well. . . .'

'Yes. However you look at it, I don't see how you can possibly wriggle out of admitting there's a contradiction here.'

Tok didn't appear to have been listening. He was standing there in the moonlight, stock-still, his arms folded, his eyes fixed firmly and serenely on the dinner table of the family of five.

After some time, he answered me, 'Well, I suppose, when you've weighed up all the pros and cons, these fried eggs are far more health-giving and hygienic than any love affair.'

*women — aggressors*

# 6

In fact, the processes and techniques of the Kappa art of love-making are very different from ours. A she-Kappa sets eyes on a he-Kappa and thinks to herself, Yes—he's the one. And from that moment on, she'll go to any lengths to make him hers, using every trick of the trade in the process. The most artless and forthright method is for the she-Kappa simply to make a mad dash for the luckless male of her choice. I've actually seen a pursuit of this sort—with a she-Kappa, looking quite out of her mind, dashing pell-mell after the male.

Sometimes, it's not just the she-Kappa alone that gives chase; she'll be joined in her hunt by her parents and even by her brothers and sisters. Fated to cope with hazards such as these, the male Kappa's lot can be a miserable one; for, even if he has the good fortune to emerge with his freedom after a skilful and drawn-out flight, it's as likely as not that he'll pay the penalty in the end, obliged to take to his bed for a rest cure that could take as long as two or three months.

I was once spending a quiet day at home, reading Tok's *Collected Poems*. Suddenly, the door opened and a figure staggered in and collapsed on the floor. It was Lap, the student. Gulping for breath, he spoke between gasps. 'My God! Caught at last! Her with her arms round me —oh, how disgusting it was.'

I flung down the anthology and rushed to turn the key in the door. Then I took a peep through the keyhole. There she was, still lying in wait outside the door; she was very tiny, her face larded quite white with powder made from sulphur.

Lap at once took himself off to my bed and lay there listlessly for several weeks. It wasn't long before his beak began to decompose; the decay ate right through it and, in the end, the beak fell away.

You mustn't think that I am trying to argue that you never see a male Kappa chasing a female for all he's worth. Of course this does happen on occasions, but these usually develop from the fact that the she-Kappa has got him worked up to the point where he just can't restrain himself a moment longer and all his passions force him to give chase.

I remember watching once as a male Kappa, almost crazed with lust, was giving chase to a she-Kappa. She was a crafty little bitch, she was; for, while making it appear, to all intents and purposes, as if she was fleeing for dear life, she would quite deliberately stop in her tracks from time to time, or try crawling along on all fours. After a good deal of this sort of play, she allowed

71

herself to be caught. The timing and the acting were quite perfect—for though the act of capture was comparatively easy, she made it seem as if it was utter exhaustion that had made her give herself up.

As I watched, the he-Kappa got her in his arms and bore her to the ground, their bodies locked in a tight embrace. They lay there together for a while. But when at last he stood up, there was a wretched look on his face that I can't quite put into words : it might have been the product of disappointment or, again, it could well have been an expression of remorse.

Whatever he felt, he was by no means as badly off as others that I heard of or saw with my own eyes.

Among the incidents I saw myself, there was one where a tiny he-Kappa was in hot pursuit after a female Kappa. She was in full flight—a flight that had all the seductive and alluring elements that a she-Kappa can express in her actions and movements. Suddenly, from a side street opposite, another male Kappa came on the scene; he was of huge build and he puffed and snorted loudly as he walked.

He could not have appeared at a more opportune moment for her; the moment she saw him, the she-Kappa let out a piercing scream.

'Help me! Help! Oh God! Help me—or else he'll kill me.'

As the she-Kappa had hoped and plotted, the well-built Kappa found it impossible to turn a deaf ear to her pleas. He made a grab at the little fellow and, in no time at all, had him flat on his back in the middle of the road. The little fellow's webbed feet clawed the air two or three times; but these were his last desperate movements and soon he sank back dead in the road.

But the she-Kappa showed not the slightest concern. By now, she had her arms locked fast round the neck of the big Kappa; the lewd grin on her face gave some hint of the pleasure she was getting from it.

Every single male Kappa I knew had been chased by a she-Kappa, almost as if by common consent. Even someone like Bag, with a wife and children, was not immune: he'd not only been chased but had actually been caught on two or three occasions. The only one I met who had never been caught was a philosopher called Mag, who lived in the house next door to Tok, the poet. One reason for this was, no doubt, that there can have been very few Kappas with such repulsive looks; and another factor may well have been that he spent practically all his time at home, hardly ever venturing out of doors.

I used to go to Mag's house occasionally for a chat. The scene was always the same; the room was dark, the shadows barely penetrated by the dim light of the seven-coloured stained-glass lantern. Mag always faced his tall-legged desk, reading the same fat books.

On one of these visits, Mag and I talked about Kappa love-making. 'Why is it that the government doesn't put much more severe restrictions on this chasing of he-Kappas by the females?'

'I suppose one reason could be that there's only a handful of females in the civil service. Female Kappas are a good deal more prone to jealousy than their male counterparts; so if only there were an increase in the number of female Kappa bureaucrats, there'd be no question that the male Kappa would live a life much freer from the risk of being pursued than he's able to enjoy as things are at present.

'However, it's patently obvious where this would all lead. With female Kappa civil servants chasing the males all over every government office, we shouldn't have got any further, you see.'

'Hm. Yes. So I suppose that, after all, the way you manage to order your life brings the greatest happiness of all.'

Mag stood up from his chair, took my hands and held them in a firm grip until he had finished his reply.

'I suppose it's only natural that you don't understand how we think about this since you aren't a Kappa yourself. Do you realize that now and again I feel the stirrings of a desire to be chased by one of those loathsome she-Kappas?'

# 7

Now and again, I used to go to concerts with Tok, the poet. To this day, I still cannot put out of my mind the third concert we went to together. Of course, there was hardly any difference between the layout of Kappa concert halls and ours in Japan. Theirs, too, had rows of gradually banked seats, and all the other things I know so well. An audience of three or four hundred he- and she-Kappas, every single Kappa-jack of them sporting a programme, used to listen earnestly and intently to each and every note.

On the occasion of this third concert, I was with Mag, the philosopher, in addition to Tok and his woman. We had seats in the very front row. After a solo 'cello piece, a Kappa mounted the stage in front of us, his score tucked nonchalantly under his arm. His narrow eyes made you feel nervous and ill at ease. This, as the programme informed us, was the famous composer, Krabach. Again, as the programme also said—but I for one had no need to consult the programme—Krabach was a

75

member of Tok's super-Kappa club, and I knew him at least by sight. '*Lied*, Krabach', read the programme. (Kappa programmes, like ours in Japan, are usually larded with a lot of German!)

In response to very warm applause, Krabach gave us the slightest of bows, and crossed to the piano with placid composure. Then, as nonchalantly as ever, he began to play a *Lied* of his own composition. In Tok's estimation, Krabach is far and away the most outstanding genius among the composers that Kappaland has produced. I was most intrigued by his music, and also by the lyric poetry that he wrote as a side-line, so I was listening closely and carefully to the notes that came from the huge arc-shaped piano. If anything, Tok (and Mag too for that matter) was perhaps even more spellbound than I.

But the beautiful she-Kappa (or beautiful, at any rate, by Kappa standards) merely kept a dumb, tight clasp on her programme, and, now and again, as if she were chafing at something, stuck out her long tongue and left it lolling at the corner of her mouth. According to Mag, this was probably something to do with her failure to catch Krabach ten years or so previously; maybe she still couldn't bring herself to regard him as anything but a sworn enemy.

Krabach, meanwhile, was soldiering on. I use the word deliberately, because he seemed almost to be at war with his piano, so much full-blooded passion did he inject into his playing. Then, all of a sudden, a voice like thunder cracked across the concert hall. 'Stop the performance!'

The shout took me so much by surprise that, unconsciously, I turned round to see where it came from. It was obviously from the quite distinguished looking policeman who was sitting in the very back row. Just as I had turned to look behind me, this policeman, lolling back sumptuously in his seat, bellowed out again, even more loudly than on the first occasion.

'Stop the performance!'

And then. . . .

And then, all hell broke loose. Shouts and screams echoed and re-echoed across the body of the hall.

'Down with police tyranny!'

'Play on, Krabach! Play on!'

'You bloody fool!'

'You filthy bastard!'

'Get out! Go on, get out of here!'

'Don't let yourself be browbeaten, Krabach. Play on!'

And while these shouts were being bandied about, chairs were up-ended, programmes flew and fluttered in all directions and, whoever threw them I've no idea, empty cider bottles, pebbles and half-chewed cucumbers rained down. Absolutely dumbfounded, I turned to ask Tok what it was all about.

But Tok, apparently quite carried away, had climbed on to his seat and kept on shrieking,

'Krabach, Krabach! Play on! Keep on playing!'

77

His excitement seemed to have infected his woman, for she, no less worked up now than he, kept screaming away :

'Police tyranny !'

At some point along the line, she had obviously quite forgotten her antipathy to Krabach.

There was no point in trying to get anything out of either of them. So the best I could do was to put my question to Mag.

'Whatever's it all about ?' I asked him.

'This you mean ? Oh, it's nothing to fuss about : it's always happening here! The essence of painting and writing. . . .'

Whenever anything sailed past him, Mag merely ducked his head slightly and, calm and undisturbed, carried on with his explanation.

'The essence of painting and writing is that it should be absolutely obvious to anyone and everyone what it is that the artist and the writer aim to give expression to. As a result, in this country we have never practised anything on the lines of a prohibition on sale or exhibition. But what we do have in its place is a prohibition on performance. After all, you see, music is a pretty dangerous thing to have around. However much it might conduce to the thorough corruption of accepted standards, a melody isn't going to mean anything to any Kappa who has no ear for music.'

'You'd say, then, that this policeman does have an ear ?'

78

'Oh dear, I'm not sure. There is an element of doubt about it, perhaps. Maybe what it is is that, as he was listening to the melody just now, he suddenly thought back to how his heart pounds away when he is sleeping with his wife!'

In the meanwhile, the uproar had grown and the scene was even more confused. Still sitting at the piano, Krabach was surveying us haughtily. But haughtiness alone was not good enough to help him take evading action against the variety of objects that were hurled in his direction from all over the concert hall. So, every two or three seconds, this carefully assumed posture had to be abandoned. Yet even so he did somehow manage, on the whole, to maintain the dignity and the presence of the grand musician as his narrow eyes flashed fiercely.

I, too, fully conscious of the danger I was in, took great pains to manœuvre myself so that Tok would act as a shield against all the flying objects. However, in spite of recognizing the dangers, I found it hard to restrain my curiosity, and couldn't stop myself from continuing, in deadly earnest, my discussion with Mag.

'Yes, but isn't that sort of censorship one of the worst forms of interference and tyranny?'

'You haven't the first idea what you're talking about! No—ours is a much more progressive censorship than you would find anywhere else! Look at Japan, for instance. There, only a month or so back, there was another case of. . . .'

At the very moment he was going to tell me, an empty bottle fell smack on Mag's head.

'Quack!' was all he said. (Quack is merely an interjection.) Then he passed out.

*Gael the capitalist*

# 8

I can't for the life of me explain it, but I found that, from the word go, I was always on the friendliest of terms with Gael, the director of a glass corporation. Gael was the capitalist to end all capitalists. And I'd venture to say that not even in this land of fat paunches was there one that sagged and bellied out quite as disgustingly as Gael's. But, when he lounged in his easy chair at home, surrounded by his wife (she was, by the way, the image of a litchi) and by his cucumber-shaped children, Gael was the picture of bliss. From time to time, I used to go out to Gael's house for dinner, in the company of either Judge Pep or Dr Chak.

And Gael would often give me introductions for visits to a great variety of factories or plants which were connected in some way either with him or with one of his many friends. Among these very different factories, the one I found to be far and away the most fascinating was that of a book manufacturing concern.

I was shown round by a young Kappa engineer. We

stopped to look at an enormous contraption driven by hydro-electric power and, once more, I found myself astonished by the advanced state of mechanization in the industries of Kappaland. I was told that the production rate in this factory was in the region of seven million. But it wasn't this volume of production that astonished me— after all, it didn't require all that much trouble to produce this sort of target in the way of books, for, in Kappaland, all they do to produce a book is to pour paper, ink and a grey-looking powder into a funnel-mouthed machine. The ingredients are fed into the machine and, in barely five seconds, they are ejected as octavos, duodecimos, royal octavos and so on.

I watched all these different sized books cascading from the machine like a torrent, and turned to ask the engineer (who was clearly extremely proud of this process which was causing me so much astonishment) what was the nature of this grey-looking powder they were using. Still standing by his sleek, shiny black machine, he replied, with a nonchalance that hinted that I was fussing about something quite trivial :

'This, you mean? Oh, it's ass-brain. All that's been done to it is that it's been dried out and then lightly pulverized. The current price for it is two or three *sen* per ton.'

Of course, I need hardly say that such manufacturing miracles are not restricted to the sphere of book production. The same sort of thing occurs also in the production of both art and music. In fact, according to what Gael

ass-brain to make books
by mass prod^n.

once told me, in an average month Kappaland sees the invention of as many as seven or eight hundred new devices of this kind. Apparently, the process of introducing mass production is going ahead at a very rapid pace. As a result, it is reckoned that no less than forty or even fifty thousand people lost their jobs recently. Even so, I had not yet come across the word 'strike' in this country, and I scoured the papers eagerly for it every morning. I thought this rather unusual and difficult to explain and on another occasion when I had been invited to Gael's house, again in company with Pep and Chak, I made an opportunity to ask why this was so.

'Oh! That's because they're all eaten up, you see!' It was Gael who replied. His words came in the most offhand way, between puffs at his after-dinner cigar.

This phrase 'eaten up' I didn't exactly understand how it was intended. But Chak, who, as usual, was wearing his pince-nez, appeared to have noticed my bewilderment, and broke into the conversation to explain Gael's words to me.

'What Gael meant was that we slaughter any worker who loses his job, and we use his flesh as meat. Look, there's a newspaper. Let's see if there's anything about it. Yes. Listen! "This month's figure for newly-unemployed reached 64,769; the price of meat has fallen in proportion".'

'And do the workers accept a situation like this without protest? After all, slaughtering them. . . .'

strikes

'It wouldn't make any difference, however much trouble they made. You see, we have a statute covering the butchery of the worker.'

These last words came from Pep, who was making a wry face at us from behind a potted mountain peach. Not unnaturally, I was quite nauseated by what I had heard. But Gael, my host (as might be expected) and even Pep and Chak as well appeared to treat this as something quite ordinary. It was Chak, in fact, who, with a smile and in a mocking tone, gave expression to their indifference :

'After all, you see, by such action, the State takes over and saves a man all the bother of suicide or death by starvation. All it is is a whiff of poison gas, so that there's no pain worth mentioning.'

'Even so, to eat their flesh as meat in such circumstances. . . .'

'Now, please, this really isn't a joking matter, you know ! If you asked Mag about it, he'd be sure to laugh his head off ! Tell me, isn't it true that, in your country, the daughters of the fourth class are sold into prostitution ? If this is so—and you're bound to admit that it is —then it's sheer sentimentality on your part to get hot under the collar about something as trifling as eating workmen's flesh as meat !'

Gael waited for a break in our argument and, when it came, he passed me one of the plates of sandwiches on the table by his side. As he offered one to me, he said, coolly :

prostitution in Japan // strikers in Kappaland

'How about these? Do take one! These are worker-meat too, you know!'

I winced—I hardly need to say so, I imagine. More than that, I turned tail and fled as fast as I could from Gael's drawing-room, only too glad to put right behind me Pep's and Chak's bantering laughter.

As it happened, there was a storm brewing that night and there was not a star in the sky as I peered up between the roofs. I made my way home through the pitch darkness and, the whole of the way, I vomited. Even against the dark background of the night, the vomit spewed forth white, white.

# 9

In spite of it all, there was no doubting that this Gael, managing director of a huge glass corporation as he was, was an extremely good mixer. From time to time, I went with Gael to his club and spent an extremely delightful evening with him there. One reason for the pleasant atmosphere was that it was far more cosy than the super-Kappa club to which Tok belonged; for another thing, while it did not contain the depth of Mag the philosopher's conversation, Gael's talk still allowed me to look in on an entirely new world—and a wide world at that. For Gael was one who would talk in a gay and lively way about everything under the sun; and, as he talked, he was always stirring his coffee with his solid gold spoon.

Anyway, to get back to my story. One very foggy night, I was listening to Gael chattering merrily away, a vase of winter roses on the table between us. I remember distinctly that the whole room, chairs and tables too, was in Secessionist style, with a thin gold rim on a white ground. Gael seemed even more elated and self-satisfied than usual, a broad smile on his face all the time. Among other things, he was telling me about the Quorax Party which had just come to power. This word 'Quorax' is yet one more of the interjections so common as proper names in Kappaland : it has no meaning, and can only be translated by some such phrase as 'Good Heavens' or 'Bless Me'.

Be that as it may, the Quorax Party stands, above all, for 'the welfare of the whole Kappa State'.

'The man at the head of the Quorax Party is a distinguished statesman by the name of Loppe. You will remember, no doubt, Bismarck's dictum—"Honesty is the best foreign policy." Well, this Loppe extends honesty even to home policy.'

'But, in Loppe's public utterances. . . .'

'Oh! Oh! Wait a minute! Listen to what I have to say first, before you butt in like this. Those speeches—surely you realize they're all a pack of lies. However, everyone realizes that they are lies, so, in the end, it no doubt boils down to the same thing as the truth. It's only you Japanese with your prejudices, you know, who would use this term "lies" in such a wholesale way. Instead, we Kappas would. . . . Oh, but let's leave that be, shall we? It's Loppe I want to talk about, not his speeches or his lies. Now, Loppe—he's in control of the Quorax Party. But there's someone behind Loppe, and in control of him—and that's Qui Qui, the president of the *Pou Fou* newspaper.'

(This word 'Pou Fou' is, again, an interjection. It has no real meaning, and if I were obliged to offer a translation, I suppose something on the lines of 'Ah' is about the nearest you could get.)

'But don't run away with the idea,' went on Gael, 'that this Qui Qui is his own boss. Not a bit of it—there's yet one more person above and beyond him, none other than the Gael you see in front of you.'

'This . . . er. . . . Oh dear, this may strike you as terribly rude, but, well, I always understood that the *Pou Fou* paper was the ally of the worker. For its president, Qui Qui, to be under your control . . . well. . . .'

'The *Pou Fou* reporters, naturally, are all for the working man, as you'd expect. But, well, you'll agree that they are influenced and controlled by their boss, Qui Qui— and Qui Qui, of course, couldn't survive without support from me.'

While he was speaking, the smile never left Gael's lips; he was toying all the time with his solid gold spoon. As I watched Gael, I felt not so much hatred of the man himself, as a deep sympathy for the wretched *Pou Fou* reporters. In spite of my not saying a word about it, Gael seemed suddenly to sense this sympathy and, as he spoke, he puffed out his already bulging paunch.

'Whatever are you thinking? Don't forget, now, that the *Pou Fou* reporter isn't always the friend of the working man. At the very least, remember, we Kappas always tend to be for ourselves—and that this "self" takes priority over anyone or anything extraneous. And, to make matters even more complex, don't forget that Gael himself even (me, you know) is under yet somebody else's thumb! Who do you think it is? It's my wife, you know! I bet you'd never have guessed—the lovely Madame Gael!' Gael burst out laughing as he said this.

'My God! What an extremely happy situation you must be in!'

'Oh! I'm content enough with it! But of course this is also something I can disclose freely in front of you—you not being a Kappa and all that. . . .'

'So what you're really trying to say is that, deep down, it's Madame Gael who keeps the tabs on the Quorax Cabinet?'

'Yes, I'm afraid that's just about it. . . . But something like that war incident of seven years ago, for instance—that goes back to a certain she-Kappa you know, without any two ways about it.'

'War? Then you have had wars here as well?'

'Of course we have! And we'll have them in the future, too, no doubt. At any rate as long as we have neighbours.'

Only then did I realize that Kappaland is not an isolated state. Gael went on to explain that it is the Otters who are the constant potential enemy, and that the Otters maintain a level of military preparedness in no way inferior to that of Kappaland. I found myself showing considerable interest in this talk of a Kappa war against the Otters. This matter of the Otter being a formidable rival of the Kappa was a new fact of which

89

the author of *An Enquiry into the Water Tiger* certainly does not appear to have been aware: and even Yanagida Kunio, the leading Japanese folklorist, in his *Collection of Mountain and Island Folk Writings* seems not to have known of it.

'I don't need to tell you that, even before the outbreak of this war, neither of our two states ever relaxed its careful and steady watch on the other. This was because each was terrified of the other. Then, during this period of preparation and nervous mutual wakefulness, one of the Otters who was a resident here paid a visit to a certain Kappa couple. The wife was scheming at the time to kill her husband. Actually he was a thoroughly bad lot. And what's more, there was probably a fair amount of inducement in the fact that her husband was covered by a juicy life insurance policy.'

'Did you know the couple?'

'Er—no! Not both of them. Only the husband, in fact. Quite a number of people, my wife among them, say that he was a no-good. But if you ask me, that's rather wide of the mark. I'd say that he was a mental case, with a pretty severe degree of persecution mania brought on by a dread of being nabbed by she-Kappas. But, to get back to my story. The wife carried out her plot and put prussic acid in his cocoa cup. Then—how she made the mistake I just don't know—she gave it to the guest, the Otter, to drink! The Otter, of course, died, and then. . . .'

'And then it led to war?'

'Yes. Because, as luck would have it, the Otter turned out to be quite distinguished—he'd been awarded some decoration, it seems.'

'Who won the war, then?'

'We did, of course! 369,500 Kappas fell nobly in the campaign. But compared with the losses the enemy suffered this was pretty negligible. Practically every piece of fur in this country is Otter. Of course, I did my little bit for the war effort, too, you know. Besides manufacturing glass, I was in charge of the movement of coal cinders to the front line.'

'Coal cinders? Whatever did they do with them?'

'Oh, made them into food, of course! You see you can be quite sure that, as long as our bellies are empty, we Kappas will get our teeth into anything under the sun!'

'E,r—please don't be angry with me for asking this; but, well . . . how about the wretched Kappas actually in the front line? In our country a scandal always arises out of this sort of thing, you see.'

'Oh yes. Here, too. Scandal and no mistake! But as long as I myself concede the fact of scandal, no one makes an issue out of it. Mag the philosopher has something about it, doesn't he? "Let a man himself admit his evil and that evil, of itself, will disappear." And there's the further consideration that, apart from the profit involved, I was ablaze with patriotism.'

Just at that point, the club steward came to our table. He bowed to Gael and then announced, in a voice which sounded just as though he were giving a recitation:

'The house next to yours is on fire, sir!'

'Oh . . . on f . . . fire?'

Gael leapt up, dumbfounded. And, of course, I too jumped to my feet. However, the steward, in a tone of complete composure, carried on:

'But the fire has already been extinguished.'

Gael's gaze followed the steward as he retired, his expression something near to a sad, tearful smile. As I looked at him in this state, I became aware that somewhere along the line I had come to detest this glass corporation director. But the Gael who was standing there was now only a common-or-garden Kappa—no longer the mighty capitalist or anything of that order—just an ordinary Kappa.

I drew one of the winter roses from the vase and put it in Gael's hand.

'But even if the fire's been put out, it must have been a dreadful shock for your wife, you know. Why don't you get back home straight away and give her this?'

'Thank you indeed.'

Gael grasped my hand; then, with a sarcastic grin breaking suddenly over his face, he continued in a low voice:

'You see, I'm the owner of the lease of the house next door to mine. All I'm due to lose out of the affair is the fire insurance!'

I still remember very, very vividly Gael's smile as he said this; it was a smile that, even if despicable, certainly was not abhorrent.

# IO

'Whatever's the matter with you? You're certainly right down in the dumps again today, aren't you?'

It was the day after the fire. Cigarette between my lips as I spoke, I was talking to Lap, the student, who was slumped in a chair in my sitting-room. His left leg draped over his right, Lap stared down at the floor vacantly and glumly, his head lolling so low that you could not even see his rotting beak.

'Lap! Come on! I was asking what the matter was.'

'Oh! What did you say? Oh—it's not all that serious, you know.'

At long last, Lap raised his head and began in a wretched snuffling whine:

'Well, it was like this. There am I looking out of the window today and, quite casually and not really meaning anything nasty, I mutter something about the fly-catching violets being in bloom. Whereupon, what does my young sister do but quite suddenly turn white with anger, doing her very best to pick a quarrel with me, and say, "So that's all you think of me is it—a fly-catching violet, am I?" And, to crown it all, Mother, who's a great one for siding with my kid sister, really piles into me, she does.'

'Why ever should your young sister find anything so disagreeable or insulting in a simple statement about fly-catching violets being in flower?'

'Well, maybe she took it in the sense of her nabbing a he-Kappa. Anyway, as if this isn't enough, my aunt, who just can't get on with Mother at all, takes it on herself to join in the squabble, so the din gets worse and worse. And, the final straw, Father, who's absolutely sodden with booze all the year round, gets to hear of the quarrel and starts doling out a thrashing to everyone regardless. With the whole bloody situation already quite beyond control, what does my kid brother do but choose this worst of all moments to swipe Mother's purse and take himself off to the flicks or somewhere. Oh God! Honestly, I'm . . . I'm bloody. . . .'

Lap buried his head in his hands. His words trailed off and he began to sob. Naturally, I felt sorry for him; but, at the same time, I don't think I could be blamed for allowing myself to think back, in a situation such as this, to Tok's scathing contempt for the Kappa family system.

I started patting him gently on the shoulder, doing what I could to console him.

'Oh, Lap, come on! This sort of thing's quite liable to happen to anyone, you know. Come on! Cheer up, and let's have a bit of spirit showing, shall we?'

94

'But. . . . Oh Christ! If only I didn't have a rotting beak. . . .'

'It's not a bit of use talking like that. You've simply got to learn to live with it, and there's an end to it. How about us going out somewhere—to Tok's, maybe? Would you like that?'

'Tok despises me so—for not being able to screw up the guts to get away from my family as he has done.'

'Mm. I see what you mean. All right then—how about Krabach's?'

After that memorable concert I had made a great friend of Krabach, so I decided that it would be a good thing if I could somehow get Lap to the house of this redoubtable musician. By comparison with Tok, Krabach lived a pretty extravagant life. I wouldn't like it to be thought from this, of course, that he lived on the same scale as a capitalist like Gael. But he did have the means that had enabled him to collect a good deal of bric-à-brac: there were Tanagra puppets and pieces of Persian pottery cluttering up the whole room; in the middle of it all stood a Turkish style chaise-longue. And usually Krabach himself would be sporting with his children underneath his own portrait.

However, today, something seemed to have gone amiss, for Krabach was sitting stolidly, his face glum and his arms clasped solemnly and tightly to his chest. And round his feet, the floor was littered with crumpled pieces of paper. Lap, in the natural course of events, was bound to have come across Krabach from time to time—in company with Tok the poet. But on this particular day, he seemed to be unnerved by the sight of Krabach in this condition and, as soon as he decently could after he had made his bow, he quietly crept away and sat down in a corner of the room.

'Krabach! Whatever's the matter?'

My question to Krabach was almost by way of a greeting.

'What's the matter, you say! Christ—these bloody fool critics! They seem to be trying to say that my lyric verse doesn't stand comparison with Tok's.'

'Yes, but you're a musician as well, and . . . and. . . .'

'Oh yes, yes. If that's all there was to it, I could stand it perfectly well. But the trouble is, you see—I think I'm right, aren't I? on top of it all, they're trying to argue that, compared with Lok, I don't even merit the title of musician!'

Lok was a musician who was often ranked with Krabach. But, sadly, I never had the opportunity of a talk with him—no doubt through his not belonging to the super-Kappa club—although I often noticed photographs of his face, with that snub beak that gives him a quite distinctive look.

'Oh, Lok's a genius all right. But, even so, his music has none of the modern passion with which your work is so richly endowed.'

'Do you honestly think so?'

'Indeed I do!'

At this, Krabach jumped up from his chair, grabbed

96

hold of the Tanagra puppet and flung it violently at the floor. Lap, looking quite horrified, let out a scream as he made to escape from the room. However, Krabach, after making a gesture to us (Lap and me) that I took to mean 'Don't be afraid', said :

'Humph! That's because, like all other laymen, you've got no ear. If the truth's to be known, I'm almost terrified of Lok, I have such respect for him. . . .'

There was a chill in his voice now.

'What? Oh, for God's sake, let's have an end to all this false modesty.'

'False modesty? Oh Christ, come off it! In any case, if there were any question of my parading my modesty, it would be for the benefit of the critics rather than for you two. I'm a genius all right! Oh yes, there's no two ways about that. It's not on this score that I'm frightened of Lok.'

'Well then, just why are you frightened of him?'

'It's something I'm not exactly sure of. Something like, shall we say, the stars that control Lok.'

'I don't get that at all, I'm afraid.'

'Perhaps you'll understand if I put it this way. I have no effect at all on Lok : whereas, somehow and at some point, he has come to have quite an influence over me.'

'Oh, come on! That's only the result of your sensitive and susceptible nature. . . .'

'I'm not so sure. Just hear me out will you—it isn't really a question of sensitivity, you see. Lok always manages to get on quietly and contentedly with the sort of work that he alone is capable of doing, whereas I'm for ever fretting away at things. From Lok's point of view, this may well seem only the tiniest of differences between us. But from my own standpoint, it sets us miles apart.'

'But, sir, there's your heroic sonata. . . .'

This was Lap speaking; it almost sounded as if he was talking to his professor.

Krabach narrowed his already thin eyes and fixed Lap with a glare of disgust.

'Oh, shut up! What do you know about it, anyway? You see, I . . . I understand Lok, understand him even better than the dogs that yap round his trouser legs!'

'Oh, come on! You must try to calm yourself down a bit.'

'If only I could take it calmly! You see this is how it always affects me. There's something—I don't know what it is but there is something or somebody—that conjures up Lok to jeer at me. Mag the philosopher knows all about this sort of thing—Mag reading his fusty old books under his stained-glass lantern.'

'How do you mean?'

'You have a look at this—it's his latest book. *Words of the Fool*, it's called.'

Krabach handed me a book. In fact, it might be nearer the truth to say that he hurled it at me. Then, with his arms folded sullenly again, he shouted at me in a surly way:

'Well, let's call it a day, shall we? I'd like you to go now!'

98

So I was out in the street yet once more with Lap who had lapsed back into his dejected silence. The street was as bustling as ever, and there were still the lines of shops under the shade of the beech trees.

We walked along in silence and with nothing particular in mind. Then, who should we bump into but Tok, the long-haired poet. When he saw us, Tok produced a handkerchief from his belly-pouch and proceeded to mop his forehead over and over again.

'Good Heavens! It's ages since we met isn't it? I was thinking I might pop in on Krabach today—it's such a long time since I've seen him.'

Thinking that it wouldn't do any good to precipitate a quarrel between these two men of the arts, I hinted to Tok in a roundabout way that Krabach was not in the very best of moods.

'Really? Oh well, then, I'll call it off. Anyway, Krabach's nerves are in a pretty poor state, aren't they? Me too—for the last two or three weeks now, I've not been able to sleep and it's got me feeling pretty low.'

'Well then, how about joining us on our walk?'

'No thanks—I think I'll let this be enough for today. Oh! Goodness!'

Tok screamed out this last word and took a tight grip on my arm. Immediately, a cold shiver ran right through his body.

'What on earth's the matter?' Lap and I both asked the question in the same breath.

'Well, you see, I thought I saw a green monkey sticking its head out of that car window over there.'

By now I was quite worried and I urged him at all events to get Dr Chak to have a look at him. But I was wasting my breath, for Tok showed no sign of allowing himself to be prevailed upon. Then he looked from one to the other of us, comparing our faces somehow suspiciously, and even blurted out :

'But I'm not an anarchist, you know. Please be sure never to forget that, if nothing more. Well then, good-bye. Do please forgive me about Chak.'

We stood idly there as we watched Tok disappear. Then we—no, it wasn't 'we'—for Lap, the student, without my noticing, had crossed to the middle of the street and there he was, legs straddling wide, peeping through his legs at every car and every single person as they passed.

Oh God ! He's gone mad too, I thought. And, shocked, I made to pull him up.

'Don't let's joke about it. Whatever is it you're trying to do ?'

Lap, rubbing his eyes, was surprisingly composed as he replied :

'No. I'm not playing any prank. No. Everything seemed so terribly gloomy that I thought I'd have a go at looking at the world the other way up. But it turns out to be just the same, after all.'

# I I

I thought you might like to read a few extracts from philosopher Mag's book, *Words of the Fool*.

The fool always believes that everyone but himself is a fool.

The reason for our love of Nature may well be not unconnected with the fact that Nature neither detests nor envies us.

The shrewdest way to live is to despise the conventions of the age while yet managing to act in such a way as not to violate these conventions at any point.

The things we would take the greatest pride in are precisely the things we do not possess.

Not a soul would raise any objection to the destruction of idols. On the other hand, at the same time, not a soul would object to being made into an idol. Yet it is the fool, the villain, the hero—he who has been blessed most richly by the gods—who may relax with the greatest ease on the idol's pedestal. (*Krabach had made a deep score with his nail against this section.*)

The ideas essential to our livelihood were burnt out three thousand years ago. No doubt all that we do is add new flames to old faggots.

Our practice is to make a habit of standing above our own consciousness.

If it were to be that good fortune accompanied suffering, and peace accompanied fatigue, then... ?

To act as the self's advocate is far more difficult than to act as another's. Let those who doubt this look at an advocate.

Pride, passion, suspicion—all offences, three thousand years ago, grew from these three. Yet, at the same time, perhaps all virtue too.

To lessen material lust is not inevitably to bring repose. To gain repose, we need also to lessen spiritual lust. (*Krabach had also left a nail mark beside this section.*)

We are less fortunate than human beings. The human being is not as highly evolved as the Kappa. (*On reading this section, I unconsciously burst into laughter.*)

'To act' is 'to be able to act'; and 'to be able to act' is 'to act'. In the final analysis, our life cannot escape from such a vicious circle. In other words, there is consistent illogicality.

After Baudelaire turned imbecile, he summed up his view of life in one simple word. The word was 'woman'. But such a word did not necessarily express the man himself. Rather, it seems, he forgot the word 'stomach' in his reliance on his genius—the poetic genius that sufficed to support his livelihood. (*Again, Krabach had left his nail mark against this section.*)

102

If we live our lives by reason, then, as a matter of course, we would negate our own existence. The fact that Voltaire, who made a god out of reason, ended his life happily indicates that a human being is not as evolved as a Kappa.

*murder + capital punishment*

# 12

The afternoon was rather colder than average. I had got thoroughly bored with *Words of the Fool* and had set out to call on Mag the philosopher.

Then, on the corner of a deserted street, I caught sight of a skinny Kappa—as thin as a gnat he was—absent-mindedly propping up the wall. Yes—there was no mistake about it—he was the one who had run off with my fountain pen!

Got him at last! I thought and yelled to a policeman —the stout, sturdy arm of the law and no mistake—who couldn't have chosen a better moment to come on the scene.

'I say! Would you just question that chap for me? He is the one who pinched my fountain pen, about a month ago now, it was.'

The policeman raised his truncheon in his right hand —Kappa-policemen carry a truncheon made of yew instead of our Japanese sabre. 'Oi, you there! Just a moment please!' he called.

I was afraid that the Kappa might perhaps take to

his heels, but, to my surprise, he walked towards the policeman, completely composed and self-possessed. In fact, his arms calmly folded, there was a good deal of haughty arrogance in the glare with which he treated both the policeman and me. However, the policeman refused to allow this to put him off; drawing his notebook from his pouch, he swiftly set about his examination.

'Name?'

'Gluk.'

'Occupation?'

'Up until just two or three days back, I was on postal delivery.'

'Right. Now, sir; according to this gentleman's testimony, you ran off with this gentleman's fountain pen. What have you to say to that?'

'Yes. I did steal it, about a month ago.'

'For what purpose?'

'I thought it would make a wonderful toy for my child.'

'And this child of yours?'

For the first time, the policeman fixed him with a sharp look.

'He died last week.'

'You carry the death certificate, I suppose?'

The skinny Kappa produced a sheet of paper from his pouch.

The policeman looked it over and then, with a broad grin, clapped him on the shoulder.

'That's all in order. I am sorry to have given you all this trouble.'

I was flabbergasted and could only stare stupefied at the policeman. And as I stared, the skinny Kappa, muttering and chuntering away, went off and left us. At length, coming back to my senses, I asked the policeman,

'Why ever didn't you take him into custody?'

'Well, he's innocent, you see.'

'Oh, but . . . surely the very fact of his stealing my fountain pen. . . .'

'Mm, but he took it to be a plaything for his child. You agree? And now, that child is dead. If you're still not satisfied with my explanation, you just check it with Clause 1,285 in the Penal Code.'

Having flung this parting remark at me, the policeman promptly brought our conversation to an end and took himself off. I decided that, under the circumstances, the only thing left for me to do was to get to Mag's house as quickly as I could; so, muttering away to myself the policeman's last words—'Penal Code, Clause 1,285'—I set off there.

Mag the philosopher loved entertaining. In fact, he had visitors that very day in his dimly-lit room : among them were Pep the judge, Chak the doctor, and Gael the glass corporation magnate. Between them, they had collected a thick tobacco haze which lay heavy under the seven-coloured stained-glass lantern.

Of course, it couldn't have turned out more fortunate for me that Pep the judge was among the visitors. I made

106

a bee-line for Pep, sat down next to him and started questioning him at once. This was just as good as, if not better than, checking on the Penal Code, Clause 1,285!

'Tell me, Judge Pep. I realize this may seem rude to you, but is it true that you don't punish the criminal in this country?'

Pep took some time before he got round to a reply: first, he took a satisfying drag at his gold-tipped cigarette and, puffing the smoke leisurely and contentedly to the ceiling, he said as though the matter was one of no weight:

'We punish the criminal, of course we punish him, even to the point of enforcing capital punishment, you know.'

'Really? But. . . . Well, listen! About a month ago, I. . . .' And I gave him all the details of the case. Then I tried quizzing him about dear old Clause 1,285.

'Er. Yes. It goes, "In the matter of any criminal act, of whatever nature, whereas posterior to the disappearance of the particular circumstances which occasioned the said offence, it shall not be permitted to take proceedings against the person or persons committing the said offence." That is to say, in your particular case, whereas the Kappa in question, at the time when the said offence was committed, was a parent, he is now no longer such. *Ergo*, his offence, too, *ipso facto*, is to be regarded as void.'

'But I must say I find this a very irrational interpretation.'

107

'Oh come! Please, let's not have any joking about a case as serious as this. Now, I grant you, it would be irrational to regard as one and the same thing "a Kappa who was a father" and "a Kappa who is a father". Ah yes—I see now what's gone wrong; by Japanese law they would be regarded as one and the same, wouldn't they? That interpretation appears quite ludicrous to us, you know! Ha ha!'

Pep threw away his cigarette and let out a wan, luke-warm smile.

Then, Chak butted into the conversation—Chak whose link with the law was of the most tenuous. Adjusting his pince-nez fussily as he spoke, Chak asked me:

'Do you have capital punishment in Japan as well?'

'Of course we do. In Japan, it's hanging.'

I was trying my best to get as much irony as I could into this reply to Chak, in order to have a dig at Pep, whose icy detachment stuck in my gullet.

'I suppose you're going to tell me that capital punishment in this country is far more enlightened than it is in Japan!'

'Naturally. Far more enlightened.'

This was Pep again—as dispassionate as ever.

'We don't have hanging or anything like it in our country. There is, I admit, the electric chair, but we reserve it for very rare and exceptional circumstances, and we do not use it in the great majority of cases. All that happens is that the title of the offence is announced to the criminal.'

'And does this, of itself, kill the criminal?'

'Yes, he dies all right. You must remember that the Kappa is far more finely tuned than you in the matter of his nervous make-up.'

'This isn't just useful in the field of capital punishment, remember. It's a method the murderer can also make use of.'

This was Gael, the director, an easy-going smile on his face, which had assumed a violet tinge from the light through the stained glass.

'I've suffered from it, you know. Why, I almost got heart failure not long ago—simply from being told by some bloody socialist that I was a robber.'

'Yes, it's far more common than you'd probably realize. There's one barrister I used to know, for example —he—well, he died of it, in fact.'

I looked round to see who had said this; it was Mag the philosopher. As always, Mag was chattering on, not looking anyone in the face, a sarcastic smile giving a bite to his words.

'Yes—he was called a frog by somebody or other. I daresay you realize what that means. To be called a frog in this country is tantamount to being called a swine. And ever after that, he spent his day thinking, I'm a frog am I? or, I'm not a frog am I? In the end, he died of it.'

'I'd say that really boils down to suicide, wouldn't you?'

'Er. Well. Indeed, the blighter who called him a frog used the term with the deliberate intention of killing him,

109

you understand. Now, in such circumstances, would this be considered suicide, looked at from your point of view?'

It happened just as Mag was asking his question. All at once, from beyond the room we were in—it couldn't have been anywhere but Tok the poet's house—there was a sharp pistol report. The bang reverberated and re-echoed, as if bounced back by the sky.

# 13

We all rushed to Tok's house. Tok lay on his back, sprawled over his potted alpine plants, his pistol clutched in his right hand; blood still spurted from the saucer on his head. Kneeling at his side, his woman was wailing and screeching loudly, her head buried deep in his breast. I helped her up and lifted her away from him. (On the whole, I find the cold, slimy Kappa skin quite repulsive and can't say that I am at all fond of having to touch it; but this wasn't the time for such qualms.)

As I lifted her, I asked : 'What on earth happened?'

'I don't quite know what happened. All I can tell you is that he was busy writing something and then, before I realized, he'd suddenly stuck the pistol to his head and let it off. Oh God, what on earth am I to do? Qur-r-r-r. Qur-r-r-r.' (Qur-r-r-r is the noise a Kappa makes when he weeps.)

'After all, Tok was always so self-centred, wasn't he?'

It was Gael, the president of the glass corporation, who

111

said this; he was speaking to Pep the judge, and shook his head in sorrow as he spoke. But Pep was too busy lighting his gold-tipped cigarette to say anything. However, Chak, who up to that point had been kneeling over Tok and examining the wound, chose this moment to announce his findings to the five of us. His bearing was too like a doctor's for words!

'There's nothing I can do for him, I'm afraid. Tok had a chronic gastric condition and this alone meant that he became depressed at the least excuse.'

'The woman said he'd been writing something, didn't she?'

This was Mag the philosopher, speaking almost to himself and, it seemed, trying to vindicate Tok. He picked up a sheet of paper from the desk and we all five craned our necks to peer at it over Mag's broad shoulder.

Come. Let us up and go
To the valley dividing this brief world,
Where the rock walls are cool,
Where the mountain stream is pure,
Where the herb-flower is fragrant.

Mag turned towards us and, with a forced and nervous smile, said:

'This is a crib of Goethe's *Mignon*, you know. In other words, Tok's suicide means that he realized he was burnt out as a poet as well.'

At this juncture, Krabach, the musician, arrived on

112

the scene in his car. He took one look at the spectacle and stood rooted in the doorway for several seconds. Then he walked over to us and almost bellowed at Mag:

'That's Tok's will is it?'

'No. It's his last poem.'

'Poem?'

Quite in control of himself, Mag handed the draft of Tok's poem to Krabach, whose hair bristled and stood on end angrily. Completely heedless of what was going on about him, Krabach eagerly set about reading the draft poem. So absorbed was he that he hardly noticed and did not properly reply to Mag's question.

'What do you make of Tok's death?'

' "Come. Let us up and". . . . Like us all, I don't know when I am to die. . . . "To the valley dividing this brief world. . . ." '

'But, when all's said and done, you were one of Tok's friends, weren't you?'

'Friend? Ah!. . . . But Tok was always a bit of a lone wolf, you see. . . . "To the valley dividing this brief world". . . . But, oh dear, Tok, unhappily. . . . "Where the rock walls are cool. . . ." '

'Unhappily? What do you mean?'

' "Where the mountain stream is pure. . . ." Yes, it goes for you all—unhappily. . . . "Where the rock walls are cool. . . ." '

From the moment we'd entered Tok's house, there had not been the slightest let-up in the woman's wailing, so, feeling sorry for her, I put my arm gently round her shoulders and led her to a sofa in the corner of the room. There was a baby Kappa there— it would be two or three —laughing away to itself, quite ignorant of what was going on. I began playing with the child, thinking this might take some of the load off the poor woman's shoulders. And as I played with it, I suddenly felt the tears forming in my eyes. During my whole stay in Kappaland, this was the first—and the last- -time I was ever to shed tears.

'Oh dear! One's bound to feel sorry for anyone who's made a home around a man as self-centred as Tok, isn't one?'

'I couldn't agree more, in that he's made absolutely no provision for the future. . . .'

This was Pep the judge—as usual, putting a light to a fresh cigarette—agreeing with Gael the capitalist. Then, to everyone's consternation, there was a loud shout from Krabach, the musician. Still clutching the draft of Tok's poem, Krabach cried, speaking to all and sundry:

'I've got it! I've just thought up an absolutely perfect funeral dirge!'

Krabach, his narrow eyes blazing, gripped Mag's hand for a second and then bounded blithely to the door. By now, of course, Kappas from the neighbourhood were thronging round Tok's house, and, so rare was the spectacle, kept coming right up to the doorway itself and peeping inside the room. But Krabach pushed his way savagely through this crowd, shoving them to both sides as he passed, and then swung himself nimbly into his car.

114

In an instant, to the accompaniment of loud back-firing, the car swept out of sight.

'I say! Hey! Do stop staring in at us like that!'

Pep the judge, acting as policeman now, pushed the crowd of Kappas back from the doorway and closed Tok's door. The room suddenly became quiet and still, no doubt on account of this. Engulfed by this sudden silence and by the stench of Tok's blood mingling with the fragrance of the flowers of the alpine plants, we discussed how best to settle the affair. But as the rest of us talked, Mag the philosopher, still staring at Tok's dead body, was absently pondering something or other. I tapped Mag's shoulder and asked:

'What is it you are thinking about?'

'Oh, this Kappa life, you know.'

'What of this Kappa life?'

'Well, when all's said and done, you see, to fulfil his life, the Kappa. . . .' Then, not a little shamefacedly, he added, in a low tone . . . 'believes somehow or other in the power of some entity outside the Kappa.'

religion – Viverism
"faith, environment &
chance"

# 14

These words of Mag's remind me that I must tell you
something about Kappa religion. Since I am a materialist,
it goes without saying that I have never once thought
really seriously about religion. However, having on this
occasion felt a certain emotion and excitement in face of
Tok's death, I fell to wondering how Kappa religion
works. So I tried at once asking Lap, the student, all
about this problem.

'Well, we have Christianity, Buddhism, the Moslem
and Parsee faiths—the lot, you know. But, when all's
said and done, I dare say that the most prevalent of them
all would prove to be Modernism—which also goes by
the name of Viverism.' (The translation 'viverism' may
well not be too accurate or appropriate. The original word
is Quemoocha : -cha, I should say, is equivalent in sense
to the English suffix -ism, while the translation of
Quemal, the original root form of Quemoo, should con-
vey not so much the simple concept of 'to live' as the
sense of 'eating rice, drinking wine and having sex'.)

'This means, does it, that you have churches and

116

temples and all that sort of paraphernalia in this country as well?'

'Now let's have no joking about it, please! You see, the Great Tabernacle of Viverism is the largest building in the whole country. Yes, how about it? Should we go and have a look at it?'

So, one warm and sultry afternoon, with clouds hanging leaden in the sky, we set out for the Great Tabernacle, Lap, as proud as Punch, leading the way.

To be sure, Lap had not exaggerated, for the edifice was a good ten times larger than the Nikolai Hall. Nor was mere size the only thing about it. The other striking feature was that this one building combined within itself just about every style of architecture you could name.

Standing in front of the Great Tabernacle and looking up at its tall pagodas and dome-like roof, even I felt a sense of something uncanny and forbidding. In fact, these pagodas and so on looked like so many tentacles pointing to and clutching at heaven.

As we stood in front of the portico (and how paltry we must have seemed in comparison with it), for a moment I had the preposterous sensation of looking up at something more like a very rare, almost monstrously great temple.

The interior of the Great Tabernacle was just as huge. Among its Corinthian columns moved herds of worshippers; but even they, in spite of their numbers, seemed just as small and insignificant as we, in face of the vastness of the edifice. Among these worshippers, we came

117

across one whose body was bent with age. Lap dipped his head slightly to him in respectful greeting and spoke courteously to him :

'Worshipful Brother, you still enjoy your wonderful good health, I see.'

The other made his bow in return and replied in the same courteous tones :

'Oh, is it not Lap? You, too, I am happy to see, are just as. . . .'

After starting to compliment Lap, he suddenly stopped in mid-speech : perhaps, at last, he had noticed that Lap's beak was going rotten.

'Er . . . well, at all events, you look very well,' he managed to continue, at long last.

'But what is it that brings you here today?'

'I am keeping this gentleman company. As you may well be aware, sir, this gentleman. . . .' And he went on to tell the old man all about me in a few rapid and fluent words. This action had more than a little of the smack of an excuse for his hardly ever showing his face inside the Great Tabernacle.

'In this connection I did wonder whether you, sir, would be gracious enough to act as guide to this gentleman. . . .' (Lap really was laying on the formality rather thick.)

The elder smiled in a lordly, magnanimous way and then, after an initial bow of greeting, he directed my attention quietly to the altar in the forefront of the compound.

'I am afraid I shall not be able to be of any great assistance to you, my good sir. However, to tell you something about ourselves : the object of worship on the part of our believers is the "Tree of Life" which stands on the altar at the front of the compound. On the "Tree of Life", as you may have perceived, grow golden and green fruits. The golden fruit we call "The Fruit of Good", the green fruit we call "The Fruit of Evil".'

I could feel the weariness of boredom creeping over me even during this short explanation; you see, the elder seemed almost to be going out of his way to drag in the old, old parables. But I hardly need remind you that I took pains to affect an outward appearance of intent interest. Even so, I couldn't help casting the occasional furtive glance inside the Great Tabernacle.

Corinthian columns, Gothic vaults, mosaic floors with a strong Arab influence, pseudo-Secessionist pews—the blending of these diverse elements produced a strangely savage beauty. But what caught my eye most of all were the busts in marble sited in the alcoves on each side of the hall. Somehow, I felt that I recognized these figures— but this, too, was hardly surprising.

The bowed Kappa elder, after he had finished his explanation of the 'Tree of Life', walked with us until we came in front of these alcoves. Then he began giving us an explanation of the figures placed in them.

'This is one of our saints—Strindberg, who was a rebel against everything. After terrible pain and suffering, he is said to have been redeemed by Swedenborg's

119

philosophy. But the fact is that he was not saved. All that happened was that, like us, he was a believer in Viverism —or it might perhaps be truer to say that he had no alternative but to believe. You should look at his *Legends*, the book this saint has bequeathed to us. He, too, by his own confession, attempted—without success—to kill himself.'

Feeling a little dejected by all this gloom, I let my eye wander to the next alcove. The figure here was a German with a bristling moustache.

'This is Nietzsche, the poet who wrote *Zarathustra*. This saint sought salvation from the superman of his own creation. But, in the end, without being saved, he went insane. On the other hand, had he not gone insane, he might never have been added to the number of the saints. . . .'

After a moment's silence the old man led us in front of the third alcove:

'It is Tolstoy in this third alcove. This saint did greater penance than any of them; for, in that he was born into a noble household, he detested displaying his hardships and sufferings in front of the public with their great curiosity. This saint strove mightily to believe in Christ, in whom, in fact, there can be no question of believing. He went further, even to the point of making a public avowal of his belief. But, in the end, in his last years, he came to the point where he could no longer endure these pathetic lies. He, too, is well known for the occasional horror he felt for the roof-beams of his study. But since

120

it has been thought proper that he be ranked among the saints, it goes without saying that he did not take his own life.'

The bust in the fourth alcove was one of us—a Japanese. As I looked on this Japanese face, I felt, as you would expect, a wave of nostalgia.

'This is Kunikida Doppo, a poet who had a vivid recognition of the humour of the coolie who hurls himself in front of an onrushing train. But there is obviously no requirement to explain to you, sir, in any further detail. So, may we look at the fifth alcove?'

'It's Wagner, isn't it?'

'Yes, it is—a revolutionary who was the sovereign's friend. Saint Wagner, in his last years, even used to say grace before he ate! Still, of course, he was a believer not so much in Christianity as in Viverism. If you go by the letters Wagner left, this lower world drove the saint to the jaws of death on any number of occasions.'

By this time, we had reached the sixth alcove.

'This saint was a friend of Strindberg. He was a French merchant turned painter, who left his wife and children to live with a thirteen- or fourteen-year-old girl from Tahiti. There was the blood of the seafaring man coursing through those thick veins, no doubt. But please look closely at his lips—there are signs, are there not, of arsenic or something of the sort there?

'Now, in the seventh alcove we have. . . . But you must be rather weary by now. So do please come with me, sir.'

In fact, I was indeed weary. So, with Lap, I followed

the elder along a gallery filled with a strong smell of incense. We entered a room which was quite small and in the corner of which stood a black figure of Venus; underneath the statue, as an offering, lay a bunch of wild grapes. I had been expecting something of the order of an austere chamber with no decoration of this kind, and the room caused me some surprise which the elder must have noticed from my expression, for before he offered me a chair he embarked on an explanation, half regretfully and half apologetically.

'You must, after all, bear it in mind that our religion is Viverism. Our deity—the "Tree of Life"—enjoins us to "live vigorously". Lap, have you ever let this gentleman see our sacred writings?'

'No, I have not. To confess the truth, I have hardly ever read any of them myself.'

Lap scratched the saucer on his head as he made this open confession. But the elder, with a smile still as gentle as ever, carried on speaking.

'Oh! In that case, you may well not understand either. Our deity created this world in a single day. Although we use the word "tree" in our term "Tree of Life", nothing is beyond its powers. And, of course, he created the female of the Kappa species. Finding existence tedious, the female Kappa began a search for the male Kappa. And our deity, taking pity on her lamentations, took her brain and made of it the male Kappa. Then, giving this Kappa-couple his blessing, he said to them, "Eat. Have union. Live life vigorously".'

In the middle of the elder's words I thought of the poet Tok. Unhappily enough, Tok, like me, was an unbeliever. In that I am not a Kappa, it's quite natural and excusable that I know nothing about Viverism. But Tok, born in Kappaland, should surely have known about the 'Tree of Life'. I had been saddened by Tok's end—Tok who had not accepted the teachings of this sect —and, by way of interrupting the elder's flow of words, I mentioned the Tok affair.

'Ah! That wretched poet, you mean, do you?'

As he listened to my account, the elder heaved a deep sigh:

'Our fate is determined by three counts—and three only—namely faith, environment and chance. You humans, of course, would no doubt wish to add heredity to this list as a fourth factor. Unhappily, poor Tok did not possess faith. Tok envied you, of that I am quite sure. As, indeed, I also envy you. And Lap—well he is still young and. . . .'

'If only my beak would mend, then things might begin to turn more rosy-coloured for me.'

As he listened to our conversation, the elder heaved yet one more deep sigh and there were tears glistening in his eyes—eyes that were fixed intently on the black Venus.

'In fact, I also—and this is my secret, known to no one, so I implore you not to divulge it in any way—I, also, in fact, cannot believe in our deity. However, sometime or other, my prayers might be. . . .'

It happened just as the elder was saying this. The door

123

of the room was suddenly thrown open and a huge she-Kappa burst in and flung herself violently upon the elder. Of course, Lap and I tried to get our arms about her and hold her back from him. But the she-Kappa was too swift for us and, in a flash, she had hurled him down on the bed.

'You old fool! You've swiped something to pay for your booze from my purse again today, haven't you?'

Ten minutes or so later—trying to make it seem that we were not running away—we had left the elder and his wife behind and were going out of the portico of the Great Tabernacle.

'With her to contend with, it's no wonder that even the elder can't bring himself to believe in the "Tree of Life".'

This was Lap speaking to me after we had walked in silence for some distance. But, instead of replying, I found myself involuntarily turning round to look back at the Great Tabernacle. Just as ever, the Great Tabernacle was stretching its tall pagodas and domes, like so many tentacles, towards a leaden, cloudy sky. Somehow, over it there hovered the eerie quality of a mirage floating in a desert sky.

# 15

A week or so afterwards, I happened to hear a rather weird story from Dr Chak. Apparently, there had been talk of a ghost appearing in Tok's house. By now, Tok's woman had taken herself off somewhere else and the house of our poet friend had been turned into a photographer's studio. The story as I heard it from Chak was that, on every photograph taken in this studio, the image of Tok was somehow or other always reflected mistily behind the picture of the actual subject.

Of course, being a materialist, Chak did not put any faith in things such as a life after death. In fact, while he was giving me an account of the story, he added, almost by way of commentary and with a smile that had a good deal of malice in it :

'It would seem, after all, that the soul does have a material existence, wouldn't it ?'

My attitude of disbelief in ghosts was not very different from Chak's. However, out of friendship for Tok the poet, I rushed straight off to a bookstall and bought every newspaper and magazine that carried a report or photo-

graph of Tok's ghost. There was evidently something in
the rumours, for when I examined the photographs, behind each subject—young or old, male or female—there
did appear, though very indistinctly, the image of a
Kappa which resembled Tok. (One couldn't quite pin-
point this resemblance, but, nevertheless, it was there.)

But, in my case, far more disturbing than these photographs were the reports about Tok's ghost and in particular a report on the affair from the Society for Psychic
Studies. I worked out a fairly close and literal version of
this Report, of which I think it might be as well to give
you the broad outlines. (Please note that those parts in
brackets are my own comments.)

REPORT ON THE GHOST OF MR TOK THE POET
(As printed in the *Journal of the Society for Psychic
Studies* Vol. 8274)

Our Society for Psychic Studies convened an Extraordinary Meeting of Enquiry at No. 251, . . . Street, the
former residence of Mr Tok, the poet, who some time
ago committed suicide, and at present used as the studio
of . . . the photographer.

The following members of the Society were present.
(*I have omitted this list of names.*)

We, the seventeen members of the Society for Psychic
Studies whose names are recorded above, together with
the President of the Society, Mr Pek, assembled at 10.30
in the forenoon of September 17th in a room at the
above-mentioned studio. We were accompanied by our

most reliable medium, Madame Hop. From the moment of entering the said studio, Madame Hop discerned a spiritual atmosphere. She suffered convulsions in her whole body and even vomited a number of times. Madame Hop herself imputed this reaction on her part to the fact of Tok's being addicted to full-strength tobacco and the resultant high nicotine content in his spiritual atmosphere.

The Society members sat in silence at a round table in company with Madame Hop. After three minutes twenty-five seconds, the medium suddenly entered into a condition of abrupt trance and became possessed by the ghost of Mr Tok the poet.

Members of the Society, in turn according to their age, commenced the following dialogue with Madame Hop while she was possessed by Tok's spirit.

QUESTION : Why do you manifest yourself as a ghost?

ANSWER : Because I wish to know what reputation I have gained since my death.

QUESTION : Do you, or do all spirits, still seek for a name for themselves after death?

ANSWER : Speaking for myself, at least, I find that I cannot stop myself craving such fame. And yet—to give you an opposite example—one poet from Japan whom I chanced to meet despises such posthumous fame.

QUESTION : Do you know the name of this poet?

ANSWER : Unhappily, it has slipped my memory. All that I can remember is a seventeen-syllable *haiku* of his—of which he was very fond.

127

QUESTION :   How does it go in translation?
ANSWER :        'An old pond
                A frog jumps in
                Splash !'
QUESTION :   Do you regard it as a good poem?
ANSWER :   No. On every count, it is a bad piece of work.
But if only the word 'frog' were altered to read
'Kappa', it would be a brilliant piece of writing.
QUESTION : What is your reason for saying this?
ANSWER :   Well, simply that we Kappas fondly hope to
see ourselves in every art form.


At this point, our Chairman Mr Pek drew the attention
of the seventeen members present to the fact that the
meeting was an Extraordinary Meeting of Enquiry of the
Society for Psychic Studies, and that its purpose had
nothing to do with critical discussion or evaluation.


QUESTION : How would you describe the features of the
life led by a spirit?
ANSWER :   They're in no way different from that led by
you.
QUESTION : If this is the case, do you feel any regrets at
having taken your own life?
ANSWER :   No, I have not the slightest regret. And if I
were to become weary of the spiritual life, I would no
doubt put a pistol to my head and bring myself back
to life again !
QUESTION :   This matter of 'bringing yourself back to
life'—is it something that is easy to achieve or not?

Tok's spirit answered this question by itself putting a further question. This, for anyone who had any acquaintance with the old Tok, was perfectly typical of his way of carrying on a conversation.

ANSWER : Is taking your own life something that is easy to achieve or not?

QUESTION : Is a spirit's span of life eternal?

ANSWER : The various theories built round our life span are so confused and contradictory that it is hard to put any credence in any of them. You should not forget, of course, that in our midst, also, there are all manner of faiths—Christianity, Buddhism, Moslemism, Parseeism and so on.

QUESTION : How about yourself—what is your faith?

ANSWER : As ever, I am a sceptic.

QUESTION : Even so, I presume that you feel no scepticism about the existence of the spirit, at least, do you?

ANSWER : Well, I find I am unable to hold the same strong conviction about it that you all have.

QUESTION : How about friends—how many do you have?

ANSWER : Oh, my friendships reach over all boundaries of time and space—they are ancient, modern, from the east and from the west. The number probably would not be far short of three hundred and, of these, if I had to name the most celebrated, I suppose it would be Kleist, Mainländer, Weininger. . . .

QUESTION : So your friends are all suicides, are they?

ANSWER : No, this is not invariably the case. A man

129

like Montaigne, who advocated and justified suicide, is one of my most esteemed friends. But I cannot bring myself to associate with fellows like Schopenhauer, the pessimist weary of life who did not kill himself.

QUESTION : Is Schopenhauer in good health?

ANSWER : At the moment, he has started something called Spiritual Pessimism, and is arguing the rights and wrongs of coming back to life. However, now he has discovered that cholera is also carried by bacteria, he seems to be very much eased.

The Society members then questioned Tok's spirit in turn, seeking information about the spirits of Napoleon, Confucius, Dostoyevsky, Darwin, Cleopatra, Buddha, Demosthenes, Dante, Sen no Rikyū and the like. It was unfortunate, however, that Mr Tok did not attempt to reply in any detail but, instead, questioned us about various items of gossip concerning Mr Tok himself.

QUESTION : What kind of name have I left after death?

ANSWER : One of the critics described you as 'among the general run of poets'.

QUESTION : He was no doubt someone who harboured a grudge against me for not presenting him with a copy of my *Collected Poems*. Has the *Complete Collection* of my poems been published yet?

ANSWER : Yes, the *Complete Collection* has been published. But it appears that sales are by no means brisk.

QUESTION : Three hundred years from now—that is, when copyright has lapsed—everyone will be sure to buy his copy of my *Complete Collection*. How about that girl she-Kappa I was living with?

ANSWER: She has become the wife of Mr Lak, the bookseller.

QUESTION: Sadly for her, she surely cannot have discovered yet that Lak has a glass eye. How about my child?

ANSWER: It is said that it is being cared for in a National Home for Orphaned Children.


Mr Tok fell silent for a while and then began his questioning afresh.

QUESTION: What has happened to my home?

ANSWER: It has been turned into a photographer's studio.

QUESTION: And what has happened to my desk?

ANSWER: No one knows what has happened to it.

QUESTION: I kept a store of treasured letters under lock and key in a drawer in my desk. But, happily for me, you gentlemen are too occupied to make them your concern. However, the dusk will be falling slowly by now in our spirit world. So I must take my leave of you, gentlemen. Good-bye, then, gentlemen. Good-bye, good people.


With these last words, Madame Hop abruptly regained consciousness.


We, the above-signed members of the said Society, on oath before God in Heaven, vouch for the authenticity of the dialogue as recorded.

We wish to record, furthermore, that we have rewarded the services of our trusted medium, Madame Hop, in accordance with the scales of the daily allowance she received during her former career on the stage.

# 16

After reading reports of this kind, I found myself becoming gradually more and more disenchanted with life in Kappaland and made up my mind to return somehow or other to the land of mankind. However, search for it as I might, I just could not discover the hole through which I had fallen.

In the meanwhile, dear old Bag, the fisher Kappa whom I had met right at the beginning, happened to mention that somewhere in the suburbs of the city there was a Kappa who lived a peaceful old age, browsing among his books and blowing idly into his flute. I wondered whether, if I were to call on him, he might be able to tell me the way to escape from Kappaland. So I went straight out to the suburbs to find him. However, in the tiniest of houses, I found, not an aged Kappa, but a young fellow, barely twelve or thirteen, not mature enough even for his head-saucer to have hardened; he was blowing into a flute serenely and contentedly. Of course I thought I must have come into the wrong house: however, just to make certain, I tried asking this young

Kappa's name. To my astonishment, for there could not have been any mistake, this was the very same aged Kappa whose name Bag had been kind enough to mention to me.

'But you look no more than a child. . . .'

'Ah! You clearly have not heard about me yet, have you? I do not know why fate dealt me this unkindness, but I had a whole head of white hair when I came from my mother's womb. Then I grew gradually younger and now, as you see, I have turned into a child. But if you count up my years—reckoning for my being sixty when I was born—I am probably all of a hundred and fifteen or a hundred and sixteen years old.'

I glanced round his room. It could have been something to do with my own frame of mind, I suppose, but there did seem to be a delightfully limpid and happy atmosphere emanating from the plain and homely chairs and table.

'You do really appear to live a much happier life than any other Kappa I know.'

'Yes—I suppose you may well be right. It may be something to do with my being old in my early years and my growing younger in my old age. Hence I am not a prey to the covetousness of the older person, nor do I wallow in the lust of the younger man. At all events, even if my life may not have been one of good fortune, it has, without any doubt, at least been peaceful.'

'Yes, of course, on these counts it must have been peaceful.'

'No—I cannot agree that such factors alone are enough to bring peace. You see, in addition, I have always enjoyed my health and never once in my life has there not been enough in my pouch-pocket for me to have a square meal. However, I do agree that the most fortunate thing of all was that I was born old.'

For a while, I talked with him about my Kappa friends—Tok who had killed himself and Gael who had his doctor in for an examination every day. I don't know why, but somehow the old Kappa did not appear to be taking a great deal of interest in what I was saying.

'It would seem that you don't appear to have the same marked attachment to life as the rest of the Kappas I know.'

The old Kappa kept his eyes steadily on my face as he replied in a quiet voice :

'But do not forget that I, too, like every other Kappa, left my mother's womb at my own volition after I had been asked by my father to decide once and for all whether or not I wished to be born into this country.'

'But I tumbled down into this country entirely by chance. And now I would ask you if you would please tell me how I could escape from here.'

'There is only one way by which you could escape.'

'And that is?'

'The way by which you came.'

My hair stood on end when I heard this reply.

'But the sad thing is that it just isn't to be found.'

With eyes young and fresh as water, the old man

135

looked at me steadily, never letting his firm gaze wander. At length, he stirred, stood up and went to the corner of the room where a rope was hanging from the ceiling. He pulled on it, to open a skylight which I had not noticed until then. Beyond the glass of the skylight, I could see pine and cypress trees and behind their spreading branches, the wide sky stretched blue and bright. And there, soaring bravely to the sky like an arrowhead, was the peak of dear old Mount Yarigatake. I found myself, in fact, jumping for sheer joy in my excitement—rather like a child that had just seen its first aeroplane.

'Well, I don't see that there would be anything wrong if you got out that way,' said the old man, nodding towards the rope as he spoke. What I had been thinking of as a rope up till then turned out in fact to be a rope ladder.

'Thank you. I shall accept your offer and leave by your rope ladder.'

'There is just one thing I might as well say to you before you go. That is, take care that you do not find yourself having second thoughts once you have left us.'

'I shall be all right on that score, never fear. There will be no such thing as second thoughts as far as I am concerned.'

I didn't leave him any time : with these words, I took firm hold on the ladder and swung myself briskly up and away—watching the saucer on the old Kappa's head grow further and further away beneath me.

*return of Gulliver*

# 17

For some while after my return from Kappaland, I used
to find myself quite unable to stomach the disgusting
smell of human beings. Compared with us, the Kappas
really are a clean-living race. Again, because I had
grown so accustomed to seeing Kappa and Kappa only,
the human head at first struck me as something terribly
weird. Perhaps you may find this rather hard to understand—but, believe you me, although there may be
nothing wrong with human eyes or the human mouth,
this protuberance we call a nose is capable, in some
mysterious way, of instilling a great deal of dread. Of
course, I tried as far as possible to meet no one; but, at
some stage along the line, I found myself gradually able
to bear the sight of human beings and, within half a year
or so, I was able to go anywhere and everywhere. Even
so, there was always one thing that gave me trouble: in
the course of a conversation, I would find myself inadver-
tently dropping back into Kappanese. It usually went
something like this:

'You will be at home tomorrow, then, will you?'

'Qua.'

'What was that you said?'

'Erm. No. I meant to say, yes. I will be at home.'

However, exactly a year after my return from Kappaland, because a business I had started came to grief. . . .

[As he started to tell me all about this ill-fated business venture, the doctor in charge warned him to leave the subject alone. The doctor informed me, in fact, that whenever he mentions this affair, he becomes so violent that even the male nurses are quite unable to keep him under control.]

Very well then, I will not take it any further. But, as I say, because a business I had started came to grief, I thought of returning to Kappaland once again. Yes—I I have chosen my words very carefully—for, you see, I think in terms not of 'going' but of 'returning' to Kappaland : for, at the time, I felt the same affection for Kappaland as I would have for my own native land.

I crept stealthily out of my house and was just on the point of getting on a Chūō Line train when, alas, I was arrested by a policeman and, after a lot of palaver, was admitted to this hospital.

For a time after coming to this hospital, I kept on thinking back to Kappaland. How is Dr Chak getting on I wonder? I'll bet Mag the philosopher, is, as ever, mulling away at something or other under his seven-coloured stained-glass lantern! And my closest friend of all, Lap, the student, with his beak going rotten. . . .

138

It was a cloudy afternoon, just like today. I was deep in these recollections when something happened that almost made me scream out loud—unknown to me, Bag, the fisher Kappa, had come into the ward and was standing there in front of me, nodding his head repeatedly to me in a Kappa bow. Once I had regained control of my heart, I can't remember now whether I wept or laughed; but what is at any rate certain, I was really touched by the simple fact that I would be able to use Kappanese again after so long an interval.

'Hey! Bag! What on earth are you here for?'

'Oh, I came up from Kappaland to visit you. There was talk of your being ill, you see.'

'However did you get to know of it?'

'They gave it out in the news on the radio.'

Bag smiled in triumphant self-satisfaction.

'Even so, you did well to get here, didn't you?'

'How do you mean? It was no trouble at all getting through to you here—the rivers and canals of Tokyo are as roads to us Kappas, you know.'

I realized—as if for the first time—that the Kappa, like the frog, is an amphibian.

'But there are no rivers around here, are there?'

'No. But I got up here through a water pipe. And after that all I had to do was to open a fire hydrant and. . . .'

'You opened a fire hydrant? How on earth?. . .'

'Oh come, sir! Surely you hadn't forgotten that we Kappas also have our share of engineers?'

This was the start of regular visits by all sorts of

Kappas; every two or three days, there'd be one in my room.

According to the diagnosis of the doctor in charge of this home, it's something called dementia praecox that I'm suffering from. But Dr Chak's opinion—which I suppose is far from being complimentary to you—is that it's not I who have got this dementia praecox, but you, the doctor in charge and all the rest of you. If there are any madmen here, it's you!

Even a Kappa as eminent as Dr Chak has taken the trouble to come up to visit me, you see. So it goes without saying that Lap the student, Mag the philosopher and the rest have been here. Bag the fisherman is the only one to have made the journey in the day-time. The rest come during the night; and a visit by a group of two or three together always occurs at night-time, when there is a moon.

Last night, with the moon shining bright, I had a delightful conversation with, among others, Gael the director of the glass corporation, and Mag the philosopher; Krabach the composer came along too and obliged with a tune on his violin.

Yes—look over there on the table! You see that bunch of black lilies—that was a present from Krabach last night.

[I turned my head and looked behind me to the table; there was no bunch of flowers—or anything—there.]

Yes, and this book too. . . . Mag brought it for me specially, last night. Just have a look at this first poem.

Oh, but of course, I'm quite forgetting that you're not likely to understand a single word of Kappanese. So let me have a go at reading it for you. This book is hot off the printing press; it's one of the volumes in the series of *The Collected Works of Tok*.

He opened a tattered telephone directory and, in a loud voice, began reading out this poem :

> In the palm flowers, among the bamboo,
> Buddha long went fast asleep
>
> With the withered fig tree by the roadside,
> Christ, too, is already dead.
>
> But we all need our rest—
> Even in front of the stage set
>
> When you look behind the set,
> You find only patched canvas.

But I'm nowhere near as pessimistic as our poet—as long as I have the occasional visitor from Kappaland.

Oh yes—this talk of visitors reminds me of one other thing I must tell you. You'll remember me talking of another of my Kappa friends, Pep the judge; well, after he'd lost his job, he went quite out of his mind. Someone told me that he's now in a mental hospital in Kappaland. If only the doctor in charge here would give his consent, it would be so nice to go and visit him. But. . . .

# Other TUT BOOKS available:

JAPANESE THINGS: Being Notes on Various Subjects Connected with Japan *by Basil Hall Chamberlain*

THE JOKE'S ON JUDO *by Donn Draeger and Ken Tremayne*

THE KABUKI HANDBOOK *by Aubrey S. Halford and Giovanna M. Halford*

KAPPA *by Ryūnosuke Akutagawa; translated by Geoffrey Bownas*

KOKORO: Hints and Echoes of Japanese Inner Life *by Lafcadio Hearn*

KOREAN FOLK TALES *by Im Bang and Yi Ryuk; translated by James S. Gale*

KOTTŌ: Being Japanese Curios, with Sundry Cobwebs *by Lafcadio Hearn*

KWAIDAN: Stories and Studies of Strange Things *by Lafcadio Hearn*

LET'S STUDY JAPANESE *by Jun Maeda*

THE LIFE OF BUDDHA *by A. Ferdinand Herold*

MODERN JAPANESE PRINTS: A Contemporary Selection *edited by Yuji Abe*

MORE ZILCH: The Marine Corps' Most Guarded Secret *by Roy Delgado*

NIHONGI: Chronicles of Japan from the Earliest Times to A.D. 697 *by W. G. Aston*

OLD LANDMARKS AND HISTORIC PERSONAGES OF BOSTON *by Samuel Adams Drake*